A JOURNEY TO EASTER

A Grandpa Joe Story

Eric C Alger

Eternal Roots LTD

FROM ASHES TO RESURRECTION

Grandpa Joe takes Danny and Hannah on a life-changing trip to Israel, retracing Jesus' steps during Lent—a special 40-day time when many Christians prepare for Easter by thinking about Jesus, praying, and sometimes giving up something they like to show their love for God. Different churches do this in different ways. For example, some have special church services, called liturgies, which are like a plan for how everyone prays, sings, and listens to Bible stories together.

During their trip to places like Bethlehem, Galilee, and Jerusalem, Danny and Hannah see where Jesus lived, taught, and performed miracles. They also learn about the important events of his life, like the Last Supper and his resurrection, and discover how people around the world celebrate this time of year in their own special ways. This journey helps them understand their faith and the meaning of Lent in a whole new way.

READING PLAN: JOURNEY TO EASTER

This reading plan follows the 40-day journey of Lent, concluding on Easter Sunday. Each day's reading aligns with a key moment from *A Journey to Easter*, offering reflection and scripture.

Week 1: Preparing for the Journey

- **Day 1 (Ash Wednesday):** A New Adventure (Genesis 3:15)
- **Day 2:** Ash Wednesday Reflections (Mark 1:15)
- **Day 3:** The First Promise (Isaiah 7:14)
- **Day 4:** Bethlehem—The House of Bread (Micah 5:2)
- **Day 5:** The Shepherds' Field (Luke 2:8-20)
- **Day 6:** The Wilderness of Judea (Matthew 4:1-11)
- **Day 7 (Sunday Reflection):** A Light in Galilee (John 8:12)

Week 2: Walking in Jesus' Footsteps

- **Day 8:** The Sea of Galilee (Mark 4:35-41)
- **Day 9:** The Mount of Beatitudes (Matthew 5:1-12)
- **Day 10:** Capernaum—The Centurion's Faith (Matthew 8:5-13)
- **Day 11:** Healing by the Water (John 5:1-15)
- **Day 12:** The Feeding of 5,000 (John 6:1-14)
- **Day 13:** The Good Shepherd (John 10:11-18)
- **Day 14 (Sunday Reflection):** The Transfiguration (Matthew 17:1-9)

Week 3: The Road to Jerusalem

- **Day 15:** Jericho—The Blind Man Sees (Luke 18:35-43)
- **Day 16:** The Road to Jerusalem (Luke 9:51)
- **Day 17:** Palm Sunday in Jerusalem (John 12:12-19)
- **Day 18:** The Temple Courtyard (Matthew 21:12-17)
- **Day 19:** Lessons from a Widow (Mark 12:41-44)
- **Day 20:** The Last Supper Room (Luke 22:14-20)
- **Day 21 (Sunday Reflection):** Washing Feet (John 13:12-17)

Week 4: The Passion of Jesus

- **Day 22:** Gethsemane—A Night of Surrender (Matthew 26:36-46)
- **Day 23:** The Arrest of Jesus (Matthew 26:47-56)
- **Day 24:** Peter's Denial (Luke 22:54-62)
- **Day 25:** The Via Dolorosa—The Way of Suffering (Luke 23:26-31)
- **Day 26:** The Crucifixion (Luke 23:33-46)
- **Day 27:** The Curtain Torn (Matthew 27:50-51)
- **Day 28 (Palm Sunday Reflection):** The Burial of Jesus (Luke 23:50-56)

Holy Week: The Victory of Resurrection

- **Day 29 (Holy Monday):** A Quiet Reflection (Isaiah 53:4-6)
- **Day 30 (Holy Tuesday):** The Empty Tomb (Luke 24:1-12)
- **Day 31 (Holy Wednesday):** The Road to Emmaus (Luke 24:13-35)
- **Day 32 (Maundy Thursday):** Thomas Believes (John 20:24-29)
- **Day 33 (Good Friday):** Jesus Appears by the Sea (John 21:1-14)
- **Day 34 (Holy Saturday):** The Great Commission (Matthew 28:16-20)
- **Day 35 (Easter Sunday):** Ascension on the Mount of

Olives (Acts 1:6-11)

PLANNING THE OVERSEAS JOURNEY

Part 1: Preparing For The Journey (Chapters 1–10)

1. **A New Adventure** – Grandpa Joe surprises Danny and Hannah with a trip to Israel for Lent.

2. **Ash Wednesday Reflections** – On the plane, Grandpa Joe explains the significance of Lent: repentance, reflection, and preparation for Easter.

3. **The First Promise** – A conversation about Genesis 3:15 sets the foundation for understanding God's redemptive plan.

4. **Bethlehem—The House of Bread** – Visiting the Church of the Nativity, they reflect on Jesus' humble birth and His role as the Bread of Life.

5. **The Shepherds' Field** – Standing where the angels appeared, Grandpa Joe shares how God reveals His love to unexpected people.

6. **The Wilderness of Judea** – Exploring the wilderness, they reflect on Jesus' 40 days of fasting and resisting temptation.

7. **A Light in Galilee** – Arriving in Galilee, they visit places where Jesus taught, healing the sick and sharing God's love.

8. **The Sea of Galilee** – A boat ride on the sea becomes the

perfect moment to retell the story of Jesus calming the storm.

9. **The Mount of Beatitudes** – Grandpa Joe teaches them about the Beatitudes and the blessings of God's Kingdom.

10. **A Personal Reflection** – In a quiet moment at sunset, Danny begins to ask deeper questions about his own faith.

Part 2: Walking In Jesus' Footsteps (Chapters 11–20)

11. **Capernaum—The Centurion's Faith** – Visiting this ancient town, Grandpa shares the story of the Roman centurion who trusted Jesus' authority.

12. **Healing by the Water** – At the Pool of Bethesda, they learn how Jesus healed the paralyzed man (John 5:1-15).

13. **The Feeding of 5,000** – Sitting near the hillside where Jesus performed the miracle, Grandpa Joe discusses God's provision.

14. **The Good Shepherd** – In a quiet valley, Grandpa shares the parable of the Good Shepherd, connecting it to Jesus' care for them.

15. **The Transfiguration** – They climb Mount Tabor, where Jesus was revealed in glory, showing His divine identity.

16. **Jericho—The Blind Man Sees** – Visiting Jericho, they recall the story of Bartimaeus' healing and the power of persistent faith.

17. **The Road to Jerusalem** – Grandpa Joe prepares them for what's coming: Jesus' final days on Earth.

18. **Palm Sunday in Jerusalem** – Walking along the Palm

Sunday road, they imagine Jesus' Triumphal Entry.

19. **The Temple Courtyard** – In the ruins of the temple, they reflect on Jesus' righteous anger and His love for God's house.

20. **Lessons from a Widow** – Visiting the site where Jesus observed the widow's offering, Grandpa Joe shares the importance of sacrificial giving.

Part 3: The Passion Of Jesus (Chapters 21–30)

21. **The Last Supper Room** – They visit the Upper Room, where Grandpa Joe explains the significance of communion.

22. **Washing Feet** – A powerful reenactment helps Danny and Hannah understand Jesus' act of humility and service.

23. **Gethsemane—A Night of Surrender** – In the Garden of Gethsemane, Grandpa shares how Jesus prayed, "Not my will, but Yours."

24. **The Arrest of Jesus** – Grandpa recounts how Jesus was betrayed by Judas and taken away by soldiers.

25. **Peter's Denial** – In a quiet courtyard, they reflect on Peter's failure and the grace Jesus offered.

26. **The Via Dolorosa—The Way of Suffering** – Walking the path Jesus carried the cross, Danny and Hannah begin to grasp the depth of His sacrifice.

27. **The Crucifixion** – Visiting Golgotha, Grandpa Joe gently tells the story of Jesus' death, emphasizing the meaning of redemption.

28. **The Curtain Torn** – They learn about the temple curtain being torn in two and what it means for our access to God.

29. **The Burial of Jesus** – Standing outside the Garden

Tomb, Grandpa shares the grief and silence that followed Jesus' death.

30. **A Quiet Reflection** – Danny and Hannah process what they've seen and heard, realizing the cost of their salvation.

Part 4: The Victory Of Resurrection (Chapters 31–40)

31. **The Empty Tomb** – On Easter morning, they visit the empty tomb and hear the words, "He is not here; He is risen!"

32. **The Road to Emmaus** – Grandpa shares how Jesus revealed Himself to two disciples after His resurrection.

33. **Thomas Believes** – Grandpa explains the story of "doubting Thomas," reminding them that faith is trusting what we cannot see.

34. **Jesus Appears by the Sea** – At the Sea of Galilee, they hear how Jesus restored Peter after his denial (John 21).

35. **The Great Commission** – Grandpa Joe shares Jesus' call to "go and make disciples of all nations."

36. **Ascension on the Mount of Olives** – They visit the Mount of Olives, where Jesus ascended into heaven, promising to return.

37. **A Promise Fulfilled** – Grandpa reminds them that every prophecy about Jesus came true, showing God's perfect plan.

38. **Danny's Questions Answered** – In a final heart-to-heart, Danny expresses his growing faith and understanding of Jesus' sacrifice.

39. **Hannah's Reflection** – Hannah shares how the trip

has helped her see God's love in new ways.

40. **Home Again, Forever Changed** – Back home, the family celebrates Easter with renewed hearts, grateful for the journey that deepened their faith.

INTRODUCTION

The wind rustled through the branches of the old oak tree as Grandpa Joe settled into his favorite chair by the fireplace. Across the room sat Danny and Hannah, wide-eyed and full of questions, just like last year when they journeyed through the story of Christmas. That season had taught them so much—how God's promises were fulfilled in the humble birth of Jesus, how love often shows up in unexpected places, and how hope changes everything.

But now, winter had melted into spring, and Grandpa Joe had another story to tell—one that reached deeper, stretched longer, and ended with the greatest triumph of all.

"This time," Grandpa said, his voice steady and warm, "we're going on a journey to Easter. But it won't just be stories told by the fire or lessons learned in our own backyard. We're going to the very places where it all happened—where Jesus walked, taught, suffered, and rose again."

Danny's eyes lit up. "We're going somewhere?"

Grandpa Joe smiled. "Yes. To Israel—the land of the Bible, where the greatest story ever told came to life."

With those words, the room seemed to shift. This wouldn't just be another series of stories; this would be an adventure of the heart, mind, and spirit. Lent, Grandpa explained, was a season of **preparation, repentance, and reflection**. It wasn't about rushing to the joy of Easter morning but about walking through the dust, the tears, and the sacrifices that made resurrection possible.

For forty days, Danny, Hannah, and Grandpa Joe would travel

through ancient streets, climb rugged hills, and stand at the foot of the cross. Along the way, they would learn what it truly meant to follow Jesus—to see His compassion, hear His truth, and witness the ultimate sacrifice of love.

And as they journeyed, perhaps they would discover something new about their own faith: that God's plan for redemption is not just a story from long ago but a living, breathing invitation for all of us today.

This book is for anyone who longs to take that same journey —to walk alongside Danny, Hannah, and Grandpa Joe as they explore the life, death, and resurrection of Jesus Christ. Through the dusty paths of Galilee to the triumphant sunrise of Easter morning, may this story bring you closer to the heart of God and to the incredible truth that **Jesus lives**.

Are you ready to begin the journey?

PART 1: PREPARING FOR THE JOURNEY

CHAPTER 1: A NEW ADVENTURE

The cold air still clung to the early morning as Grandpa Joe sat at the kitchen table, his Bible open in front of him. Sunlight filtered through the window, casting golden streaks on the worn pages. It was a familiar scene—one Danny and Hannah had grown used to seeing—but this morning felt different, as if something important was about to happen.

"Good morning, Grandpa!" Hannah said, bounding into the kitchen. Danny followed close behind, a sleepy yawn escaping as he dropped into the seat across from Grandpa Joe.

"Good morning, you two!" Grandpa said, closing his Bible gently. His deep voice carried a kind of peace, the way it always did when he spoke about things that mattered. "You're just in time."

"For breakfast?" Danny grinned, looking toward the stove.

Grandpa Joe chuckled and leaned back in his chair, his eyes bright with excitement. "No, for something even better. How would you two like to take a trip this year? A trip that could change your lives forever."

Danny and Hannah froze.

"A trip?" Hannah asked. "Where to?"

"To the land where Jesus walked. To Israel." Grandpa's words hung in the air for a moment, heavy with meaning. "We'll be walking through the very places where the greatest story of all time unfolded. It's time we took a journey to Easter."

Danny frowned a little, rubbing the sleep from his eyes. "A journey to Easter? But we already know the story, Grandpa. Jesus died and rose again. What more is there?"

Grandpa Joe's gaze softened, and he placed a hand on the Bible before him. "Oh, there's so much more, Danny-boy. You see, we often rush to Easter morning without stopping to take the journey that gets us there. Lent is a season of preparing our hearts, of repentance, and of reflection. It's a season where we're reminded that the cross came before the empty tomb. And sometimes," he paused, "we need to take a walk in the footsteps of Jesus to truly understand the price He paid and the love He poured out for us all."

Hannah's eyes widened. "We're going to see all of that? Where it really happened?"

Grandpa nodded. "That's right. From the quiet fields of Bethlehem, where His life began, to the busy streets of Jerusalem, where He carried the cross. We'll stand in the wilderness where He was tempted and sit by the Sea of Galilee where He taught. Every step will remind us of God's love, God's plan, and God's victory."

As Grandpa Joe spoke, it felt as though the room itself had grown still, as if the Spirit of God was pressing truth into their hearts. That was the way Grandpa spoke about Jesus—with reverence, with joy, and with a certainty that made everything feel real and alive.

Danny shifted in his seat. "But Grandpa... why do we have to go to those places to understand it?"

Grandpa's face broke into a smile as he leaned forward, his voice dropping slightly, steady and clear. "Because sometimes we need to *see* before we can truly believe. Jesus invited people to *come and see* who He was. And even now, He calls us to come closer, to look deeper, to walk with Him."

He paused, holding their gaze. "God's love isn't something far off or hard to find, Danny. It's real. It's personal. And it's for you.

That's what Easter is all about."

The room fell silent again. For a moment, the only sound was the quiet ticking of the old clock on the wall.

Finally, Hannah broke the silence, her voice small but hopeful. "I want to go, Grandpa. I want to see it all."

Danny glanced at his sister, then back at Grandpa. "Me too."

Grandpa Joe beamed, his heart full. "Well, then. We'll pack our bags and prepare our hearts. This is more than just a trip—it's a journey of faith. And as we walk, we'll learn together what it means to follow Jesus all the way to the cross… and beyond."

He stood, his voice filled with the kind of conviction that had shaped generations of preachers and believers alike. "Remember this, children—Easter is not just a story of death and resurrection. It's a story of love, of sacrifice, and of victory. A victory that can change your life, if you'll let it."

As Danny and Hannah left the kitchen to begin packing, Grandpa Joe turned back to the window, his eyes lifting toward the morning sky.

"Thank You, Lord," he whispered softly. "Thank You for the cross. And thank You for this journey."

Outside, the world was waking up, unaware of what was to come. But in Grandpa Joe's heart, the promise of Easter already shone bright—a light in the darkness, a hope that would never fade.

CHAPTER 2: ASH WEDNESDAY REFLECTIONS

The hum of the plane's engines filled the cabin as Grandpa Joe leaned back in his seat, his Bible open in his lap. Danny and Hannah sat beside him, a little restless but wide awake with excitement.

"Grandpa," Danny asked, adjusting his seatbelt, "what's Lent again? You said it's about Easter, but what are we supposed to do for 40 days?"

Grandpa looked over at Danny and smiled, his voice steady but soft, the way he always spoke when sharing something important. "Lent is a season of repentance, reflection, and preparation. It's about looking at our hearts—seeing where we've fallen short—and turning back to God."

Hannah tilted her head, "Why 40 days, Grandpa?"

"That's a great question," Grandpa said, his face lighting up. "The number 40 shows up all over Scripture. Moses spent 40 days on the mountain with God. The Israelites wandered in the desert for 40 years. And Jesus—He spent 40 days in the wilderness, fasting and praying, preparing for His ministry."

"What was He preparing for?" Danny asked.

Grandpa looked at him intently. "For you, Danny. And for me. For all of us." He held up his Bible, his fingers brushing its worn edges. "Jesus knew what was ahead—temptation, suffering, and the cross. But He also knew why He had come: to save us from our sins. And He prepared His heart by drawing closer to His Father."

Danny sank back into his seat, thoughtful. "Why do we have to reflect and repent? I mean, I haven't done anything *that* bad…"

Grandpa Joe smiled kindly, his eyes gentle. "Oh, Danny-boy, none of us like to think about the wrong we've done. But Lent isn't about making us feel ashamed—it's about drawing closer to God. You see, when we recognize our sin, it points us to how much we need a Savior. Without understanding our need, we'll never fully appreciate what Jesus did for us on the cross."

Hannah sat quietly, staring out the window at the clouds stretching endlessly below them. "It sounds… kind of hard, Grandpa."

"It is," Grandpa said honestly. "Looking at our hearts takes courage. But it's also beautiful because when we turn back to God, He meets us with open arms. Lent prepares us to celebrate Easter—not just the empty tomb, but the journey that took Jesus to the cross."

He paused, flipping gently to a verse in his Bible. "David once prayed, *'Create in me a clean heart, O God, and renew a right spirit within me.'* That's the heart of Lent—a prayer that God would cleanse us and draw us closer to Him."

****

The three of them sat in silence for a while, the quiet hum of the plane filling the space between them. Danny glanced over at Grandpa's Bible and then back at his own reflection in the window.

"Do you think it works?" he finally asked. "Like, do you think God really hears us?"

Grandpa turned to him, his eyes bright with certainty. "Oh, I know He does. God's Word says, *'If we confess our sins, He is faithful and just to forgive us.'* That's a promise, Danny. And God never breaks His promises."

Hannah reached over to take Grandpa's hand. "Can we start now, Grandpa? Can we ask Him to clean our hearts?"

Grandpa nodded, his voice filled with quiet joy. "We sure can, sweetheart. Let's pray together."

As the three of them bowed their heads, the soft murmur of their prayer rose above the hum of the plane. It was just a small moment—high in the sky, far from home—but it marked the beginning of their journey.

A journey that would take them to the cross. And beyond.

CHAPTER 3: THE FIRST PROMISE

The sky was streaked with orange and pink as the day began to wane. Grandpa Joe led Danny and Hannah to a quiet bench in a small garden just outside their guest house in Jerusalem. The garden was peaceful, filled with olive trees whose twisted branches seemed to hold secrets of centuries past.

"Sit down, kids," Grandpa said, patting the worn wooden bench. "Before we continue this journey, I want to take us back to the very beginning. To the moment when God first gave us the promise of a Savior."

Danny furrowed his brow. "You mean Jesus?"

"Yes," Grandpa replied. "But long before Jesus was born in Bethlehem, God spoke about Him. He gave us a promise—a *first promise*—that He would send someone to defeat sin and evil."

Hannah leaned forward. "Where's that in the Bible?"

Grandpa opened his Bible to the very first book—*Genesis*. The familiar pages seemed to glow in the soft evening light. "It's in Genesis 3:15," he said. "This was after Adam and Eve disobeyed God in the Garden of Eden. They listened to the serpent instead of trusting God, and sin entered the world."

He read slowly, his voice steady and clear:

'And I will put enmity between you and the woman, and between your offspring and hers; he will crush your head, and you will strike his heel.'

Danny looked confused. "What does that mean? Who's

crushing whose head?"

Grandpa smiled gently. "That verse is sometimes called the *first gospel* because it's the first time God promises to send a Savior. It's a prophecy. God was speaking to the serpent—the devil—when He said that one day, the offspring of the woman would crush his head. That 'offspring' is Jesus."

****

The words hung in the air for a moment. Hannah glanced at Grandpa, her curiosity piqued. "So, the serpent strikes Jesus, too? Like... hurts Him?"

"Yes, Hannah," Grandpa said, his voice softening. "That's the cross. The devil thought he had won when Jesus was crucified, but it was only a bruise to the heel. Three days later, Jesus rose from the grave, crushing sin and death once and for all. He won the ultimate victory."

Danny's eyes widened as he let the words sink in. "So, God had a plan all along? Even from the beginning?"

"That's exactly right," Grandpa said, his face lit with joy. "God didn't abandon us when sin entered the world. He made a promise—a promise of redemption. The moment humanity fell, God already had a plan to lift us up."

****

For a while, they sat quietly, the olive trees swaying gently in the breeze. The sun dipped lower, casting long shadows across the garden.

"Grandpa," Danny said after a long pause, "if God promised to send Jesus right away, why did it take so long for Him to come?"

Grandpa's gaze lifted to the sky. "God's timing is not like ours, Danny. The Bible says, *'With the Lord a day is like a thousand years, and a thousand years are like a day.'* God was preparing the world for Jesus' arrival. Every story in the Old Testament points to Him —Abraham, Moses, David, the prophets. They all showed pieces of God's plan until, in the fullness of time, Jesus came."

Hannah hugged her knees close to her chest. "It's like a puzzle," she said quietly. "Each piece matters."

Grandpa nodded. "Exactly. God's plan of redemption is perfect. And Genesis 3:15 is the first piece of that puzzle. It reminds us that even when we stumble, even when we fall, God does not leave us. He is always working to restore us to Himself."

****

As the light faded, Grandpa closed his Bible and smiled at the children. "Now, let me ask you something," he said. "What does this promise mean to you?"

Danny was the first to answer. "It means God had a plan to save us even when we messed up."

"And it means He loves us enough to send Jesus," Hannah added.

Grandpa Joe beamed with pride. "That's exactly right. The First Promise isn't just about a story from long ago—it's about all of us. God sent Jesus to crush sin and bring us back to Him because of His great love."

The three of them sat there as the first stars began to shine above the olive grove. Danny and Hannah didn't say much as they walked back to their room that night, but their hearts were full. For the first time, they were beginning to see that Easter wasn't just about Jesus' death and resurrection—it was about a promise made long ago. A promise kept.

And a promise that changed everything.

CHAPTER 4: BETHLEHEM—THE HOUSE OF BREAD

The sun was warm as it climbed higher over Bethlehem. The streets bustled with vendors, tourists, and local families going about their day, yet there was something timeless about the air. It felt like a place where history and holiness met, where the world slowed down just enough to remember something sacred.

Grandpa Joe led Danny and Hannah down a stone-paved path toward the **Church of the Nativity**. The ancient building loomed before them, its weathered walls whispering stories that stretched across centuries.

"This is it," Grandpa Joe said, his voice reverent. "The place where Jesus was born."

Danny tilted his head, looking up at the church's façade. "*Here? In this big stone building?*"

Grandpa Joe chuckled softly. "Not quite like this, Danny-boy. Long ago, before this church was built, there was a quiet cave —humble and dark. That's where it happened. That's where the Savior of the world entered into our brokenness."

Hannah's face lit up with curiosity. "A cave? Why not a palace? Why would God let His Son be born in a place like that?"

Grandpa Joe stopped walking and looked at the two of them, his eyes kind and full of meaning. "Because God wanted us to see something important, Hannah. Jesus wasn't born for kings and queens alone. He was born for *everyone*—rich and poor, the forgotten and the outcast. He came to meet us in our need, not in our pride."

****

Inside the church, the air was cool and hushed. Voices dropped to whispers as light poured through the small windows, reflecting off the stone walls. Grandpa Joe led Danny and Hannah to a section where visitors knelt and touched a silver star embedded into the ground.

"This," Grandpa said quietly, pointing, "is believed to mark the very spot where Jesus was born."

Danny and Hannah knelt beside Grandpa, their eyes wide with wonder. Danny reached out a hesitant hand, his fingertips brushing the cold stone.

"It doesn't look like much," he whispered.

Grandpa Joe smiled faintly. "No, it doesn't. But you see, that's the beauty of it, Danny. The King of Kings came into the world in the humblest of places. The Bible says, *'He had no beauty or majesty to attract us to Him.'* Jesus didn't come with trumpets or golden thrones. He came as a baby, wrapped in swaddling cloths, lying in a manger."

Hannah looked up, her voice thoughtful. "But why, Grandpa? Why *here*?"

"Because Bethlehem is the perfect place for God's plan," Grandpa said gently. "Do you know what 'Bethlehem' means?"

Hannah shook her head.

"It means **'House of Bread.'**"

Danny sat up straighter. "Bread? Like the kind we eat?"

"Yes," Grandpa said, his face softening with joy. "And that's not by accident. Jesus would one day call Himself the *Bread of Life.*" He paused, his voice steady and full of meaning. "Just as bread nourishes our bodies, Jesus came to nourish our souls. He came to fill the emptiness in our hearts that nothing else can satisfy."

****

The three of them sat for a while in silence, the whispers of prayers rising around them. Hannah glanced at the families and pilgrims kneeling nearby, some wiping tears from their eyes.

"Do you think they're praying for something?" she asked softly.

Grandpa Joe nodded. "I think so, Hannah. Many people come here carrying burdens they can't bear alone. Some come in gratitude, some come with grief. But no matter why they're here, Jesus meets them—just like He meets us. He is the Bread of Life because He gives us what we need most: forgiveness, peace, and eternal life."

Danny's face grew serious. "Why do we need forgiveness, Grandpa? I mean, we're not bad people…"

Grandpa turned to him, his voice low but firm. "Danny, it's not about being good or bad. The Bible says, *'All have sinned and fall short of the glory of God.'* That means every single one of us has turned away from God at some point. But Jesus—born in Bethlehem, in the House of Bread—came to offer us a way back to Him. His life, His death, and His resurrection give us hope and make us right with God."

Hannah glanced at the star again, her voice a whisper. "So, He's like… a gift?"

Grandpa Joe's eyes twinkled. "Yes, Hannah. The greatest gift of all."

****

As they stepped back outside, the sunlight hit their faces, and the sounds of Bethlehem filled the air once more—children laughing, merchants calling out, and church bells ringing faintly in the distance.

Grandpa Joe stopped and turned back to look at the church, his voice thoughtful. "You know, children, the people of Bethlehem didn't know what was happening that night. They were busy. The inn was full. But in that quiet cave, God's greatest miracle was unfolding. And it's the same today. In the busyness of life, we can miss Him. That's why Lent matters—it's a time to stop, to reflect, and to remember what Jesus has done for us."

Danny squinted up at the clear blue sky. "So, we need to make room for Him?"

"Yes," Grandpa said, smiling. "We need to make room for Him in our hearts. Because when we do, we'll discover that He is everything we've ever needed."

As they made their way back down the narrow streets, Danny and Hannah were quiet, their hearts full of the story they had just heard. Jesus, born in Bethlehem—the Bread of Life, the King who came for the world—felt a little closer now.

And as they walked, the sound of church bells echoed through the air, as if the very stones of Bethlehem were singing: *"Unto us a Savior is born."*

CHAPTER 5: THE SHEPHERDS' FIELD

The sun hung low over the hills outside Bethlehem, casting golden light across the quiet fields. The air was still, and the only sounds were the occasional bleating of sheep and the soft rustle of the wind through the dry grass. Danny and Hannah followed Grandpa Joe down a narrow dirt path, their shoes kicking up small puffs of dust as they walked.

"Where are we now?" Danny asked, squinting into the distance.

Grandpa Joe stopped and turned, leaning on his walking stick as he looked out over the open fields. "This," he said with a smile, "is where the angels appeared to the shepherds on the night Jesus was born. It's called the Shepherds' Field."

Danny looked around at the rocky slopes and low stone walls. "It doesn't seem very special," he said, frowning.

"That's exactly the point, Danny-boy," Grandpa said, his voice warm but steady. "The place itself wasn't special, but what happened here changed the world forever. It's one of the most beautiful parts of the Christmas story—and it tells us something incredible about God."

****

They walked a little farther until Grandpa led them to a small stone overlook. Below, the fields stretched out, dotted with olive trees and clusters of grazing sheep. Grandpa Joe pointed with his walking stick.

"Imagine this," he began, his voice filled with wonder. "It's a quiet night. The shepherds are out here, watching over their flocks, just like they did every other night. These weren't rich men, or powerful leaders—they were shepherds. Simple, humble people doing their jobs. And yet, on that night, God sent angels to *them*."

Hannah's eyes widened. "Why shepherds? Why not kings or priests?"

Grandpa smiled. "Because God's love doesn't depend on status, Hannah. It doesn't matter if you're rich or poor, famous or forgotten. God reveals Himself to those who are ready to hear Him. The shepherds weren't too busy, too proud, or too distracted to notice the miracle."

He opened his Bible and began to read, his voice carrying over the quiet fields:

"And there were shepherds living out in the fields nearby, keeping watch over their flocks at night. An angel of the Lord appeared to them, and the glory of the Lord shone around them, and they were terrified. But the angel said to them, 'Do not be afraid. I bring you good news that will cause great joy for all the people. Today in the town of David a Savior has been born to you; He is the Messiah, the Lord.'"

Grandpa paused, his eyes lifting from the page. "The glory of God shone all around them—imagine that! Light brighter than the sun breaking into the darkness. And the angel told them the greatest news ever given: 'A Savior has been born to *you*.'"

****

Danny sat down on a low stone wall, his brow furrowed. "To *them*? But they were just shepherds."

"Yes," Grandpa said, nodding. "And that's what makes it so powerful. God was showing the world that His Son didn't come for the important or the privileged. He came for *everyone*. The angel said the good news was for 'all people.' That means kings and beggars, leaders and servants, and even shepherds in the middle of nowhere."

Hannah sat beside Danny, looking up at Grandpa. "So, God doesn't care if we're... unimportant?"

"Not one bit," Grandpa said, his voice growing tender. "The world may overlook people like the shepherds, but God doesn't. In fact, He often chooses the ones the world forgets to do His greatest work. Look at David—before he became a king, he was a shepherd in these same fields. And look at Jesus—He was born in a manger, not a palace."

Danny looked out across the fields, his voice quiet. "I guess it means anyone can know God, then. Even us."

Grandpa Joe smiled broadly. "Yes, Danny. Especially us. The Bible says, 'God chose the foolish things of the world to shame the wise; God chose the weak things of the world to shame the strong.' The shepherds remind us that God doesn't call the perfect or the powerful—He calls the willing. And He reveals His love to those who are ready to receive it."

****

For a moment, the three of them sat quietly, the wind brushing gently against their faces. Hannah looked up at Grandpa. "What do you think the shepherds did when the angels left?"

Grandpa's voice softened with awe. "They ran to see Jesus. The Bible says they hurried to Bethlehem to find the baby, just as the angels had said. And when they saw Him lying in the manger, they couldn't keep the news to themselves. They told everyone what had happened, and people were amazed."

Hannah's eyes sparkled. "So, they became the first people to tell others about Jesus?"

"That's right," Grandpa said. "God didn't send His message to kings or priests first—He sent it to shepherds. They were the first to hear the good news, and they were the first to share it. It reminds us that when we encounter Jesus, we can't help but tell others."

****

As the sun began to dip lower in the sky, Grandpa Joe stood and stretched, his walking stick tapping against the ground. "The shepherds' story is simple, but it's a reminder to all of us: God's love is for everyone. And just like the angels called the shepherds that night, He's calling each of us to come to Jesus."

Danny and Hannah followed Grandpa as they began walking back toward the path.

"Grandpa," Danny said suddenly, "if the angels showed up here, couldn't they show up anywhere?"

Grandpa Joe turned, his face full of joy. "Oh, absolutely, Danny-boy. God can meet us wherever we are—in fields, in churches, in our homes, or even when we feel alone. All we have to do is listen and respond, just like the shepherds."

Hannah looked back one last time at the fields, her voice quiet but sure. "I hope I would have run to see Him, too."

Grandpa smiled as he placed a hand on her shoulder. "Me too, Hannah. Me too. And we still can—because Jesus isn't far away. He's as close as our hearts."

As they walked, the last light of day stretched across the fields, painting them gold. The hills were quiet again, as if waiting for the sound of angels singing:

"Glory to God in the highest heaven, and on earth peace to those on whom His favor rests."

CHAPTER 6: THE WILDERNESS OF JUDEA

The sun was blazing high as Danny, Hannah, and Grandpa Joe stepped out of the van and into the vast, rugged expanse of the Judean wilderness. Miles of rocky hills and dusty paths stretched out in every direction under a cloudless blue sky. There was no sound except the wind brushing softly across the barren land, carrying with it the stillness of a place untouched by time.

"This is it," Grandpa Joe said quietly, leaning on his walking stick as he surveyed the land. "The Wilderness of Judea. The very place where Jesus spent forty days and forty nights fasting and praying before He began His ministry."

Danny kicked at the loose gravel beneath his feet. "It's so empty," he said, his voice echoing faintly. "Nothing but rocks and dirt."

"Exactly," Grandpa replied, his voice steady and reverent. "It's a place of isolation, of quiet. It's a place where you can't hide from yourself—or from God."

Hannah looked up at Grandpa, shielding her eyes with her hand. "Why did Jesus come here, Grandpa? What was He doing all alone for forty days?"

Grandpa Joe's face softened as he turned toward them. "Jesus came here to prepare for what was ahead. He was about to begin His ministry—to teach, to heal, to show the world who He truly was. But before He could do that, He came to this wilderness to draw close to His Father and to face the devil's temptations head-on."

Danny frowned. "Why did the devil tempt Him? I mean… He's Jesus, right?"

"Yes," Grandpa said with a nod, "but Jesus was also fully human. The Bible tells us that He felt hunger, pain, and weakness, just like we do. The devil came to Him when He was tired, hungry, and alone—at His weakest point. But Jesus stood firm because He trusted God completely."

****

The three of them climbed a small ridge, and when they reached the top, Grandpa gestured to the vast emptiness before them. "Imagine Jesus standing here," he said, his voice low but strong. "For forty days, He ate nothing. He prayed, He listened to His Father, and He prepared His heart. Then, at His weakest moment, the devil came to Him and said, *'If You are the Son of God, tell these stones to become bread.'*"

Danny looked down at the rocks scattered across the ground. "Why didn't He do it? He could have made bread, right?"

"Yes, He could have," Grandpa Joe said, his voice firm. "But Jesus knew something important: the devil wasn't just testing His hunger—he was testing His trust in God. Jesus answered, *'Man shall not live on bread alone, but on every word that comes from the mouth of God.'*"

Grandpa picked up a small stone and turned it over in his hand. "You see, Danny, the devil tempts us with things we think we need—things that seem harmless or even good at first. But temptation tries to make us doubt God, to take matters into our own hands instead of trusting Him. Jesus knew that His Father would provide for Him, even when He was hungry, even when He felt weak. He trusted God's Word completely."

****

Hannah sat on the edge of the ridge, her legs dangling over the side. "What else did the devil do?" she asked, her voice quiet.

Grandpa sat beside her, brushing the dust off his pants. "The devil took Jesus to the highest point of the temple and said, *'If You are the Son of God, throw Yourself down.'* He even quoted Scripture, saying that angels would catch Him. But Jesus saw through the devil's tricks. He answered, *'Do not put the Lord your God to the test.'"*

Hannah wrinkled her nose. "That sounds like a trap."

"It was," Grandpa agreed. "The devil tried to twist God's Word to get Jesus to prove who He was. But Jesus didn't need to prove anything. He trusted God's plan. He knew who He was, and He knew what He had come to do."

"What happened next?" Danny asked, his voice eager.

Grandpa's gaze grew serious. "The devil showed Jesus all the kingdoms of the world and said, *'All this I will give You if You will bow down and worship me.'"* He paused, his voice heavy with meaning. "The devil offered Jesus power, glory, and an easy way out—without the cross. But Jesus answered, *'Away from me, Satan! For it is written: Worship the Lord your God, and serve Him only.'"*

****

The wind swept through the wilderness, rustling the dry grass at their feet. Grandpa Joe looked at Danny and Hannah, his face thoughtful. "Jesus faced every temptation we face—hunger, pride, and the desire for power or comfort. But He overcame them all because He trusted His Father completely. He didn't fight the devil with His strength—He fought him with Scripture, with truth. And He won."

Danny sat cross-legged in the dust, looking up at Grandpa. "So, what does that mean for us?"

"It means that when we're tempted, we can do what Jesus did," Grandpa said. "We can hold on to God's Word. The Bible says, *'No temptation has overtaken you except what is common to mankind.*

And God is faithful; He will not let you be tempted beyond what you can bear.' God always provides a way out."

Hannah looked down at the stones scattered across the ground. "So, we just have to trust Him?"

Grandpa nodded, his voice firm yet gentle. "Yes, Hannah. Trust Him, even when it's hard. Even when the wilderness feels lonely. Jesus showed us that God is enough—His Word, His promises, and His love will sustain us through anything."

****

The three of them sat together, the wilderness stretching endlessly before them. Grandpa Joe's words seemed to linger in the air, carried by the wind.

"You know," Grandpa said finally, "the wilderness isn't just a place on a map. We all face wilderness moments—times of struggle, loneliness, and temptation. But just like Jesus, we're never alone. God is with us, even here."

Danny picked up a small stone and held it tightly in his hand. "I don't want to face the wilderness, Grandpa."

Grandpa Joe placed a comforting hand on his shoulder. "None of us do, Danny. But it's often in the wilderness that we hear God's voice most clearly. It's where we learn to rely on Him. And when we do, we'll discover that His grace is enough to see us through."

As the sun began to dip lower in the sky, they stood and began walking back down the ridge, their shadows stretching long behind them. Danny and Hannah didn't say much as they walked, but the silence felt full—like something precious had settled deep within them.

Grandpa Joe's voice broke the stillness as they neared the van. "Remember this, children: the same Jesus who walked in the wilderness walks with us today. When you feel weak, when temptation comes, you can turn to Him. He's already won the battle."

Hannah glanced back at the hills one last time, the vastness of it all suddenly not so empty anymore.

And as they climbed into the van, Danny whispered under his breath, almost to himself, "I think I get it now, Grandpa. Jesus was never really alone. And neither are we."

CHAPTER 7: A LIGHT IN GALILEE

The morning mist hung low over the hills as the van wound its way through the narrow roads leading into Galilee. The land was green and alive, with olive groves stretching out in the distance and small villages nestled between the hills. Hannah leaned her head against the window, watching the scenery pass by, while Danny tapped his fingers rhythmically against his knee.

"This place looks so different from the wilderness," Hannah said softly.

Grandpa Joe smiled, his hands resting on his walking stick as the van bumped along. "It is different, Hannah. Galilee is a place of life and light. It was here, in these hills and villages, that Jesus began to teach and heal—spreading hope where there had been darkness."

Danny looked up. "Why here, Grandpa? Why not in Jerusalem, where all the important people were?"

Grandpa Joe's eyes twinkled. "That's the beautiful part, Danny. God often chooses the humble places and unexpected people to show His glory. Galilee wasn't where kings or religious leaders gathered. It was where fishermen, farmers, and families lived. And yet, this place would shine with the light of Jesus' love."

****

They stopped in a small fishing village along the Sea of Galilee. The water stretched out like glass under the pale blue sky, with the hills rising gently in the distance. Fishermen worked along the shore, untangling nets and pulling small boats onto the sand, much as they would have done in Jesus' time.

"This," Grandpa Joe said, stepping out of the van, "is where Jesus called His first disciples—ordinary men who were going about their day, never expecting that their lives were about to change forever."

Danny and Hannah followed him onto the shore, their shoes crunching over the pebbles. "Who were they, Grandpa?" Hannah asked.

"Peter, Andrew, James, and John," Grandpa said, pointing toward the sea. "They were fishermen, casting their nets and working hard to provide for their families. Then Jesus came to them and said something incredible: *'Come, follow me, and I will send you out to fish for people.'*"

Danny wrinkled his nose. "Fish for people? What does that mean?"

Grandpa Joe chuckled softly. "It means Jesus was calling them to something greater—to share God's love with others and to bring people into His Kingdom. You see, they were fishing for fish to fill people's stomachs, but Jesus wanted them to bring people to Him to fill their hearts."

****

They stood by the shore for a moment, the gentle waves lapping at their feet. Nearby, a small group of tourists sat quietly as a local guide retold the same story Grandpa Joe had just shared.

"Did they follow Him right away?" Hannah asked.

"They did," Grandpa said. "The Bible says they left their nets immediately and followed Him. Think about that—no hesitation, no excuses. They saw something in Jesus that was worth leaving everything behind."

Danny stared out at the water, watching a lone fisherman row his small boat farther out to sea. "Why did they trust Him like that?"

Grandpa's voice softened. "Because when Jesus calls, His words carry truth and power. These men didn't just hear a teacher —they heard the voice of God calling them to a new purpose. And as they followed Him, they saw His light spreading through Galilee."

****

Later that afternoon, they walked up a hill that overlooked the Sea of Galilee. The view was breathtaking—green hills rolling down to meet the water, the sunlight sparkling on the waves. Grandpa Joe motioned for them to sit under the shade of an olive tree.

"This is where Jesus taught many of His most important lessons," Grandpa said, sitting on a large rock. "Here in Galilee, He shared the truths of God's Kingdom—truths that turned the world upside down."

"Like what?" Hannah asked, brushing a strand of hair from her face.

Grandpa opened his Bible, flipping the pages carefully. "Let me read to you from the Sermon on the Mount. Jesus said:

'You are the light of the world. A town built on a hill cannot be hidden. Neither do people light a lamp and put it under a bowl. Instead, they put it on its stand, and it gives light to everyone in the house. In the same way, let your light shine before others, that they may see your good deeds and glorify your Father in heaven.'"

Hannah's eyes lit up. "He said *we're* the light of the world?"

"Yes, He did," Grandpa replied, his voice warm. "Jesus came as the Light of the World, shining God's truth and love into the darkness. And when we follow Him, He calls us to reflect that light—to live in a way that shows others who He is."

Danny frowned, deep in thought. "But sometimes the world feels pretty dark, Grandpa. What good is a little light?"

Grandpa Joe smiled, his eyes twinkling. "Oh, Danny-boy, even the smallest light can drive back the darkness. When you shine the love of Jesus—through kindness, forgiveness, and faith—God can use your light to change lives. Jesus didn't come to Galilee to seek out fame or power. He came to heal the sick, to feed the hungry, and to bring hope to the broken. And He calls us to do the same."

****

They sat quietly for a while, the sound of the wind rustling the leaves above them. Hannah finally broke the silence. "Did people believe Him, Grandpa? Did they see His light?"

"Some did," Grandpa Joe said, his voice thoughtful. "They saw Him heal the sick, feed the hungry, and even raise the dead. But others rejected Him because they didn't understand who He was. That's still true today. Some people hear about Jesus and open their hearts, while others walk away. But no matter how people respond, the light of Jesus keeps shining."

Danny leaned back against the tree trunk, staring out at the sea below. "I want to shine like that," he said quietly. "I want people to see Jesus in me."

Grandpa Joe smiled, his heart full. "That's a prayer God loves to answer, Danny. When you follow Jesus, His light will shine through you, even in the darkest places."

****

As the sun began to dip low on the horizon, they made their way back down the hill, their footsteps slow and thoughtful. Grandpa Joe's voice carried softly on the breeze.

"Remember this, children: Jesus didn't just bring light to Galilee. He brought light to the whole world. And that light still shines today—through His Word, through His Spirit, and through His people. You are never too young, too ordinary, or too small to let that light shine."

Hannah looked at the first stars beginning to twinkle in the deepening sky. "I want to be a light too, Grandpa."

Grandpa Joe smiled, his voice quiet but full of conviction.

"Then keep your eyes on Jesus, Hannah. Follow Him, trust Him, and let His love shine through you. Because when you walk with Him, you'll never walk in darkness."

And as they walked back to the van, the last rays of sunlight stretched across the Sea of Galilee, as if to remind them that the Light of the World had come—and He was still shining.

CHAPTER 8: THE SEA OF GALILEE

The sun glistened on the surface of the Sea of Galilee, its rippling waters stretching out to meet the rolling hills on the horizon. The air was calm and warm, carrying the faint scent of water and reeds. Danny and Hannah stood by the edge of the shore, their shoes sinking slightly into the pebbled sand as they stared at the small wooden boat tied to a post nearby.

"Are we really going out in that?" Danny asked, eyeing the boat with a mixture of curiosity and hesitation.

Grandpa Joe chuckled, his hands resting on his walking stick. "Yes, we are, Danny-boy. You can't come all this way to Galilee and not sail where Jesus sailed. Don't you worry; the boat will hold."

The boatman—a kind-faced man with tanned skin and weathered hands—waved them aboard. Soon, the boat rocked gently as they pushed away from the shore, its wooden hull creaking as it floated farther out onto the water. Danny grabbed the edge tightly, his knuckles turning white, while Hannah sat beside Grandpa Joe, grinning at the adventure.

Grandpa looked out over the water, his voice carrying both reverence and joy. "This is the same sea where Jesus taught, where He walked on the waves, and where He calmed the storm. It was here that His disciples learned a lesson they would never forget—about faith, trust, and the power of God."

****

The boat glided smoothly across the water, the hills and

distant villages growing smaller. For a while, no one spoke. The stillness of the sea seemed to hush all words, as if inviting them to listen to something greater than themselves.

Finally, Grandpa Joe broke the silence. "Do you know the story of Jesus calming the storm?"

Danny nodded hesitantly. "I think so... but I don't remember all of it."

"Well, let me tell it to you," Grandpa said, his voice taking on the steady, confident tone that always seemed to calm their hearts. "It happened on a day just like this—calm and peaceful. Jesus and His disciples were out on the Sea of Galilee, sailing to the other side. Jesus, exhausted from teaching and healing all day, fell asleep in the back of the boat."

Hannah leaned forward, her eyes fixed on Grandpa. "He was sleeping?"

"Yes, Hannah," Grandpa said, smiling faintly. "Jesus was fully God, but He was also fully human. He knew what it felt like to be tired. So, while the disciples were keeping watch, Jesus rested."

Grandpa paused, his eyes scanning the water around them, as though he could see the story playing out right in front of him. "But suddenly, a furious storm swept over the sea. The wind roared, the waves crashed, and the boat began to fill with water. These men—many of them fishermen who knew the sea well—were terrified."

Danny glanced nervously at the water, imagining the storm. "Didn't they try to save themselves?"

"Oh, they did," Grandpa said, nodding. "But no matter how hard they worked, they couldn't control the storm. In their fear, they woke Jesus and cried out, *'Lord, save us! We're going to drown!'*"

"What did Jesus do?" Hannah asked, her voice barely above a whisper.

Grandpa Joe turned to look at her, his voice steady and clear.

"Jesus stood up, looked out at the raging storm, and said, *'Peace! Be still.'*"

He paused, letting the words settle over the children like the calm after a storm. "And immediately, the wind stopped. The waves grew still. The sea became as calm as it is right now."

****

The boat rocked gently as if on cue, the water smooth and quiet beneath them. Danny looked around, as though expecting something miraculous to happen. "Just like that? The storm stopped?"

"Just like that," Grandpa said, his voice soft but filled with conviction. "And do you know what Jesus said to His disciples? He asked, *'Why are you so afraid? Do you still have no faith?'*"

Hannah frowned. "But they were in a storm! How could they not be afraid?"

Grandpa Joe smiled, his eyes full of kindness. "That's a good question, Hannah. The disciples looked at the waves and the wind, and they let fear take over. But Jesus wanted them to see something greater—something deeper. He wanted them to know that when He is with them, they have nothing to fear."

Danny glanced at Grandpa, his brow furrowed. "But why didn't He stop the storm sooner? Why did He let them get scared?"

Grandpa nodded thoughtfully, letting the question hang in the air for a moment. "Sometimes, Danny, God allows storms in our lives to show us something about ourselves—and about Him. The disciples learned that day that Jesus wasn't just a teacher or a healer; He had authority over the wind and the waves. He was, and still is, the Son of God. And even when the storm raged, He was right there with them."

****

The boat drifted slowly as Grandpa Joe's words sank in. The gentle lapping of the waves seemed almost like a response to the story—whispering, *"Peace... be still."*

"I think we're all like the disciples sometimes," Grandpa continued, his voice soft. "We see the storms in our lives—the struggles, the fears, the things we can't control—and we panic. We cry out, 'Lord, save us!' And He does. Maybe not always the way we expect, but He does. Because He's with us, even when we can't see Him at work."

Hannah looked out over the water, her face thoughtful. "So... we just need to trust Him?"

"Yes, Hannah," Grandpa said gently. "That's the heart of it. Trust Him. Jesus didn't promise that life would be free of storms, but He did promise that He would never leave us."

Danny looked up, a small smile breaking across his face. "And if He can calm the sea, He can handle anything, right?"

Grandpa Joe smiled, his heart full. "That's right, Danny. There's no storm too big, no problem too great, and no fear too strong for Jesus to handle. When He speaks, even the wind and the waves obey Him. And when we trust Him, we'll find peace—no matter how fierce the storm."

****

As the boat turned back toward shore, the sun dipped lower in the sky, painting the water in soft hues of gold and orange. Danny and Hannah sat quietly, their eyes on the horizon as the gentle waves carried them along.

For the first time in a long time, Danny felt something settle deep within him—a calm, steady peace, like the water that stretched out around them.

And as Grandpa Joe rested his hands on the side of the boat, he looked up to the sky, his voice barely more than a whisper. "Thank You, Lord, for being our peace in every storm."

The boat glided to shore, the sand crunching softly beneath its hull. The children climbed out, glancing back at the still, quiet sea as if they were leaving behind something sacred.

"Did you feel that?" Hannah asked Danny as they walked up

the beach.

"What?"

"The peace," she said simply.

Danny grinned and nodded. "Yeah. I think I did."

Grandpa Joe walked beside them, his walking stick tapping rhythmically against the sand. "Never forget, children—when life's storms come, the One who calms the sea walks beside you. Trust Him, and you'll always find peace."

And as they headed back toward the village, the Sea of Galilee sat calm and still behind them, a reminder of the Savior who speaks peace into every storm.

CHAPTER 9:
THE MOUNT OF
BEATITUDES

The path up the hillside was gentle, winding its way through wildflowers and olive trees swaying in the breeze. From the top, the Sea of Galilee stretched out in every direction, its waters shimmering beneath the mid-morning sun. Danny stopped for a moment, resting his hands on his knees.

"This is higher than I thought," he said, breathing hard.

Grandpa Joe chuckled, his walking stick tapping against the rocky path. "Well, Danny-boy, the climb may feel long, but trust me—it's worth it. This hill we're on? It's called the Mount of Beatitudes. It's where Jesus gave one of His greatest teachings: the Sermon on the Mount."

Hannah's voice carried a hint of wonder as she looked up. "So, Jesus stood here?"

"Yes, Hannah," Grandpa Joe replied, his eyes scanning the peaceful hillside. "The Bible tells us that Jesus sat down on a hill like this one and began to teach the people who had gathered. Men, women, children—rich and poor alike—they all came to hear Him speak."

As they reached the top, the three of them stood quietly, looking down at the soft slopes that rolled toward the water below. A small stone church stood nearby, surrounded by gardens full of blooming flowers. The air felt still, almost holy, as if the words Jesus spoke so long ago still lingered on the breeze.

****

Grandpa Joe motioned for Danny and Hannah to sit on a low stone wall beneath the shade of an old tree. He took out his Bible, the worn pages flapping slightly in the breeze.

"Do you know what the word *beatitude* means?" he asked, looking at the children.

Hannah shook her head, while Danny shrugged. "Not really," Danny said.

"It means *blessing*," Grandpa explained. "The Beatitudes are a list of blessings that Jesus shared with the people. But these blessings were different from what anyone expected."

"What do you mean?" Hannah asked, leaning forward.

Grandpa Joe smiled gently. "Most people think of blessings as wealth, success, or comfort. But Jesus turned that idea upside down. He showed that God's Kingdom isn't like the kingdoms of this world. His blessings are for those who are humble, hurting, or hungry for righteousness. It's not about what you have; it's about who you are in God's eyes."

****

He opened his Bible and began to read, his voice steady and clear, as if each word carried the weight of eternity:

"Blessed are the poor in spirit, for theirs is the Kingdom of Heaven."

"Poor in spirit?" Danny interrupted. "What does that mean?"

Grandpa lowered his Bible, his gaze meeting Danny's. "It means recognizing that we need God. When we're 'poor in spirit,' we know we can't do life on our own. We depend on God for everything."

He continued: *"Blessed are those who mourn, for they will be comforted."*

Hannah looked up, her brow furrowed. "How can mourning be a blessing? Mourning sounds... sad."

"It does, Hannah," Grandpa said softly. "But Jesus was showing us that God meets us in our grief. He comforts us when we're hurting. When we mourn over our sin, over what's broken in the world, God's love brings us hope and healing."

****

Grandpa Joe's voice carried on the wind as he read the next verses:

"Blessed are the meek, for they will inherit the earth. Blessed are those who hunger and thirst for righteousness, for they will be filled."

He looked at the children, his eyes kind and full of conviction. "The world teaches us to be strong, to fight for what we want. But Jesus says the meek—the gentle, the humble—will inherit God's promises. And those who hunger for righteousness, who long to see God's goodness and justice in the world, will be satisfied."

"What about the rest?" Danny asked, glancing down at the Bible.

Grandpa Joe smiled, his voice lifting as he read:

"Blessed are the merciful, for they will be shown mercy. Blessed are the pure in heart, for they will see God. Blessed are the peacemakers, for they will be called children of God. Blessed are those who are persecuted because of righteousness, for theirs is the Kingdom of Heaven."

The words settled over them like a soft blanket, carried by the quiet breeze.

****

"Grandpa," Hannah said after a moment, "why would being persecuted be a blessing? That sounds scary."

Grandpa Joe nodded thoughtfully. "It does sound scary, Hannah. But Jesus was teaching that when we live for Him, there will be times when others misunderstand us, criticize us, or even hurt us. Yet even then, we are blessed—because we belong to Him. The Kingdom of Heaven is our reward."

Danny tilted his head, staring out at the sea below. "So, these blessings... they're not really about being happy, are they?"

Grandpa's face lit up with a smile. "That's right, Danny. The Beatitudes aren't about fleeting happiness. They're about joy—joy that comes from knowing God and living in His Kingdom, no matter what happens around us. The world says you need power, riches, or fame to be blessed, but Jesus says true blessing comes when our hearts are right with Him."

****

For a moment, the three of them sat in silence, letting the words settle into their hearts. The view from the hill seemed endless, as if the very land itself was stretching toward heaven.

"Do you think people understood what He meant?" Hannah asked softly.

Grandpa Joe's eyes grew thoughtful. "Some did. Others didn't. But that's the beauty of Jesus' words—they're simple enough for a child to understand, yet deep enough to challenge the wisest person. The Beatitudes show us how to live differently—how to be people of light in a world of darkness."

Danny looked up at Grandpa. "Do you think we can live like that? Like the people Jesus described?"

Grandpa smiled, his voice gentle but sure. "Not on our own, Danny-boy. But with God's help, we can. Jesus doesn't just tell us what to do—He gives us the strength to live it out. And when we live the way He calls us to, we become a blessing to others."

****

As they stood to leave, Grandpa Joe placed a hand on each of their shoulders, his voice quiet but filled with purpose.

"Children, the Beatitudes remind us that God's ways are not the world's ways. When you feel small, overlooked, or weak, remember this: *you are blessed.* God sees you, He loves you, and He promises to be with you every step of the way."

Hannah smiled faintly. "It's like being on this hill, isn't it? You can see so much more from up here."

Grandpa Joe nodded. "That's exactly right, Hannah. The Beatitudes give us a higher perspective—a glimpse of God's Kingdom. And when we live with that perspective, we bring His light to others."

As they walked back down the hill, the sun sparkled on the Sea of Galilee, and the breeze carried a sense of peace. Danny and Hannah didn't say much, but in their hearts, the words of Jesus echoed like a promise:

"Blessed are you…"

And somewhere deep inside, they began to understand that His blessings were not just for long ago—they were for *them,* right here and right now.

CHAPTER 10: A PERSONAL REFLECTION

The sun hung low over the horizon, casting a golden glow across the Sea of Galilee. The water rippled gently, shimmering like liquid gold, while the hills in the distance seemed to soften in the fading light. Danny sat on a flat stone near the shore, his arms wrapped around his knees, staring quietly at the waves as they lapped against the shore.

Grandpa Joe and Hannah had wandered farther down the shoreline, their voices soft and distant. For the first time on this journey, Danny found himself alone—just him and the stillness of the evening.

The quiet settled over him, heavy but not uncomfortable. The questions he had carried for days—questions he hadn't known how to voice—started to bubble to the surface, pressing at his heart. He picked up a small stone and tossed it into the water, watching the ripples spread outward.

****

Grandpa Joe's voice broke the silence as he approached, his footsteps soft on the rocky shore. "A penny for your thoughts, Danny-boy?"

Danny glanced up and shrugged. "I don't know, Grandpa. I've just been thinking, I guess."

Grandpa lowered himself onto a nearby stone, leaning forward on his walking stick. "Thinking is good. Sometimes God speaks to us most clearly when we're still enough to listen."

For a long moment, neither of them spoke. The quiet wasn't awkward—it was the kind of silence that allowed space for something deeper.

Finally, Danny broke it, his voice small but steady. "Grandpa, do you ever wonder... why God would care about us? I mean, we're just people. We mess up all the time."

Grandpa Joe's face softened, and he turned his gaze toward the water. "Oh, I've wondered that many times, Danny. I think every believer asks that question at some point. But the answer always takes me back to one simple truth: God loves us—not because of who we are, but because of *who He is.*"

Danny looked up, his brow furrowed. "What do you mean?"

"I mean that God's love isn't something we earn, Danny. It's who He is. The Bible says, *'God is love.'* From the moment He created us, He's been reaching out to us, calling us back to Himself. And even when we fail, even when we fall short, His love doesn't change. That's why Jesus came."

Danny picked up another stone and rolled it between his fingers. "But why *me*? Why would God care about someone like me?"

****

Grandpa Joe leaned closer, his voice steady and warm, filled with the same conviction that had guided generations of believers. "Danny, let me tell you something. God doesn't see you the way you see yourself. You see your mistakes, your questions, your weaknesses. But God sees a child He loves deeply. He sees your potential, your heart, and your future. And He cares about you so much that He sent His Son to save you."

Danny looked down at the stone in his hand. "But what if I don't feel like I deserve it?"

Grandpa smiled gently. "None of us deserve it, Danny. That's the beauty of grace. God's love isn't about what we deserve—it's about what He's done for us. Jesus didn't wait for us to be perfect; He came while we were still broken. He took our sin and shame to the cross, and in exchange, He gave us forgiveness and new life."

Danny stared at the water, his thoughts turning over in his mind. The ripples spread farther and farther, like the questions in his heart. "Grandpa, how do you *know* all of this is true? I mean… how do you really know?"

Grandpa Joe's voice dropped to a whisper, but it carried the weight of a lifetime of faith. "Because I've seen what God has done in my life, Danny. I've felt His presence in the darkest nights and in the brightest days. I've seen His faithfulness when I didn't deserve it. And I've heard His voice in moments just like this—quiet, still, calling me to trust Him."

****

The wind stirred softly, carrying the scent of the water and the sound of distant birds returning to their nests. Grandpa Joe placed a hand on Danny's shoulder.

"Danny, faith isn't about having all the answers. It's about trusting the One who does. It's about knowing that God loves you, even when you have questions. Even when life feels uncertain, He is certain. And He's inviting you to trust Him."

Danny sat quietly for a moment, Grandpa's words sinking into his heart. "I don't know if I have enough faith, Grandpa."

Grandpa Joe smiled, his eyes twinkling with kindness. "Do you remember the story of the mustard seed?"

Danny shook his head.

"Well," Grandpa said, "Jesus told His disciples that faith as small as a mustard seed can move mountains. A mustard seed is tiny—just about the size of the tip of your finger. But it grows into something strong. That's all God asks of us, Danny—to bring Him the little faith we have and let Him do the rest."

Danny looked up at Grandpa, his voice soft but sure. "Do you think I could have faith like that?"

Grandpa nodded, his voice gentle. "I know you can, Danny. Faith isn't about how much you have; it's about *who* you put it in. When you trust Jesus, even with the smallest seed of faith, He will strengthen you. He will show you that He's real, that He's good, and that He loves you."

****

The sun dipped lower, painting the sky with streaks of orange and pink. Hannah's laughter echoed in the distance as she skipped stones farther down the shore. Danny stood up, brushing dust from his jeans, and looked out across the water one last time.

"I think I want to try, Grandpa," he said quietly. "I want to trust Him."

Grandpa Joe stood as well, his face beaming. "That's all God asks, Danny-boy. Bring Him what you have, and He'll take care of the rest."

They began walking back up the shore, the quiet rhythm of the waves behind them. Danny slipped the small stone into his pocket, as if holding onto something precious—something that reminded him of the mustard seed Grandpa had spoken of.

And as the sun finally disappeared beyond the hills, Danny felt something new settle in his heart—a whisper of hope, a flicker of faith. It wasn't big, but it was real.

And for now, that was enough.

PART 2: WALKING IN JESUS' FOOTSTEPS

CHAPTER 11: CAPERNAUM—THE CENTURION'S FAITH

The town of Capernaum sat nestled along the shore of the Sea of Galilee, its ruins whispering of the lives once lived in this ancient place. Sunlight glinted off the remnants of stone houses and narrow streets as waves lapped gently nearby. Danny and Hannah followed Grandpa Joe along the uneven paths, their footsteps crunching softly on the gravel.

"This place feels... different," Hannah said quietly, looking at the ancient synagogue ahead. "Like something really important happened here."

Grandpa Joe stopped and turned to face them, leaning on his walking stick as a smile lit his face. "You're right, Hannah. Capernaum was an important place during Jesus' ministry. He taught in this very synagogue. He performed miracles here. And it's where we learn about one of the most remarkable displays of faith in the entire Bible."

"What kind of faith?" Danny asked, squinting against the bright sun.

"The faith of a Roman centurion," Grandpa Joe replied, his voice steady and filled with wonder. "A man who understood something that even some of Jesus' own people struggled to grasp—Jesus' authority."

****

They stepped into the ruins of the synagogue, the smooth stone still standing tall in places. Grandpa Joe motioned for Danny and Hannah to sit on a low wall while he stood before them, his Bible open in his hands.

"Let me tell you what happened," Grandpa began, his voice carrying with quiet power. "Jesus had returned to Capernaum after traveling and teaching, and word had spread that He was there. People brought Him the sick, the hurting, and the broken. Everyone wanted to see Jesus."

He paused, his eyes sparkling with excitement as he continued. "But one day, a Roman centurion—a commander of a hundred soldiers—sent some men to Jesus with a request. His servant, someone he cared deeply for, was gravely ill and about to die. Now, a centurion was a powerful man, a Roman officer who could order people to come and go as he pleased. Yet, this man turned to Jesus."

Hannah tilted her head. "Why would a Roman officer go to Jesus? I thought the Romans didn't like Him."

Grandpa Joe nodded. "That's what makes this story so powerful, Hannah. The centurion wasn't a Jew. He didn't grow up hearing the promises of the Messiah. But something about Jesus—His reputation, His authority, and His compassion— made the centurion believe that Jesus could heal his servant."

Danny sat up straighter. "What did Jesus do?"

Grandpa's voice softened. "At first, Jesus started toward the centurion's home. But before He got there, the centurion sent another message: *'Lord, don't trouble Yourself, for I do not deserve to have You come under my roof. That is why I did not even consider myself worthy to come to You.'*"

Danny frowned. "Wait... He didn't want Jesus to come to his house?"

Grandpa smiled and held up his hand. "Not because he didn't believe. Listen to what he said next: *'But say the word, and my servant will be healed.'* The centurion understood something extraordinary—he knew that Jesus didn't need to be physically present to perform a miracle. All He had to do was speak, and it would be done."

****

The sunlight filtered down through the broken walls of the synagogue as Grandpa Joe's words hung in the air.

"Jesus was amazed," Grandpa said, his voice low with reverence. "The Bible tells us that Jesus turned to the crowd following Him and said, *'I tell you, I have not found such great faith even in Israel.'* And do you know what happened next?"

Danny shook his head, eyes wide.

"The centurion's servant was healed at that very moment," Grandpa said, his voice lifting with joy. "Without Jesus laying hands on him, without seeing Him face-to-face. Jesus spoke, and it was done. The centurion had trusted Jesus' word completely."

****

For a moment, the three of them sat in silence, the ancient stones around them seeming to bear witness to the story. Finally, Hannah spoke. "Why did Jesus say the centurion's faith was so great?"

Grandpa Joe smiled gently. "Because the centurion understood what many others missed—Jesus' authority. He believed that Jesus' words carried power, just like a Roman officer's commands. But this was more than human authority. The centurion recognized that Jesus was sent by God, and with that authority, nothing was impossible."

Danny looked down at his shoes, kicking a small pebble. "Do you think we can have faith like that, Grandpa?"

Grandpa Joe nodded, his voice firm. "Oh yes, Danny. Faith like that is possible for anyone who trusts in Jesus. The centurion didn't have all the answers. He didn't have a lifetime of Bible knowledge. But he believed in Jesus' power and love—and that's what made his faith so strong."

****

The three of them stood and began walking back toward the shore, the sound of seagulls filling the quiet space. Grandpa Joe stopped suddenly and looked out over the water.

"You know," he said, his voice thoughtful, "this story teaches us something about the heart of God, too. Jesus could have ignored the centurion. He could have said, 'You're not one of my people.' But He didn't. Jesus saw his faith, and He responded. That's the kind of Savior we have—One who looks at our hearts, not at where we come from or who we are."

"So Jesus cares about everyone?" Hannah asked, walking alongside him.

"Everyone," Grandpa replied, smiling. "No one is too far from His love or His power. The centurion was a Roman soldier, yet Jesus met him in his need. And He will meet us in ours, too. All we have to do is trust Him."

****

As they reached the shore, the Sea of Galilee shimmered under the afternoon sun. Danny and Hannah sat on the sand, their eyes on the water.

"Grandpa," Danny said suddenly, "what if I'm like the centurion—if I don't feel worthy enough for Jesus to help me?"

Grandpa Joe placed a hand on Danny's shoulder and knelt beside him. "None of us are worthy on our own, Danny. But Jesus doesn't ask us to be. The Bible says, *'It is by grace you have been saved, through faith—and this is not from yourselves, it is the gift of God.'* Jesus' love and power aren't things we earn; they're gifts we receive by faith."

Hannah looked out at the sea, her voice quiet but certain. "So, we just need to trust Him?"

Grandpa Joe smiled. "That's right, Hannah. Faith as small as a mustard seed is enough to move mountains because it's not the size of our faith that matters—it's the One we put our faith in."

****

As the sun dipped lower in the sky, the three of them sat quietly, letting the lessons of the day settle deep in their hearts. The waves brushed gently against the shore, as if echoing the power of Jesus' words:

"Say the word, and my servant will be healed."

And as Danny watched the water ripple outward, he realized that trust—true trust—wasn't about what he could see. It was about believing that Jesus' words were enough.

And for the first time, he felt ready to try.

CHAPTER 12:
HEALING BY
THE WATER

The air was still and heavy with the hum of the city as Grandpa Joe, Danny, and Hannah made their way through Jerusalem. The narrow streets wound their way between ancient stone walls, carrying echoes of voices from generations past. The group finally stopped before a site where two large pools, lined with broken columns and arches, lay beneath them.

"This," Grandpa Joe said softly, "is the Pool of Bethesda."

Danny and Hannah leaned over the railing, staring down at the ruins. The pool was dry now, but the arches and steps leading into it seemed to whisper stories of long ago. The sunlight cast shadows across the uneven stones, as if time itself had paused to remember what had happened here.

"It doesn't look like much," Danny said, squinting. "It's all broken."

Grandpa Joe smiled faintly, resting his hands on his walking stick. "You know, Danny, sometimes the most broken places are where God's greatest miracles happen. This pool may look empty now, but once, it was a place of hope and healing. And it's where Jesus revealed the heart of God in a way that changed everything."

****

They found a quiet spot near the edge of the ruins, where

Grandpa Joe opened his well-worn Bible. The sound of distant city life faded as he began to read:

"Now there is in Jerusalem near the Sheep Gate a pool, which in Aramaic is called Bethesda and which is surrounded by five covered colonnades. Here a great number of disabled people used to lie—the blind, the lame, the paralyzed."

Grandpa paused, looking up at Danny and Hannah. "This was a gathering place for those who had nowhere else to turn. The sick and the suffering would come here and wait, hoping for a miracle. You see, there was a belief that from time to time, an angel would stir the waters, and whoever stepped in first would be healed."

Hannah's brow furrowed. "But what about the people who couldn't move fast enough? What happened to them?"

Grandpa's face grew solemn. "They waited, Hannah. Day after day, year after year. Imagine the despair—watching others find hope, while you felt forgotten. That's where we meet a man in this story, a man who had been paralyzed for thirty-eight years."

Danny sat up straighter, his voice filled with wonder. "Thirty-eight years? That's longer than you've been alive, Grandpa!"

Grandpa laughed gently. "Well, *almost* longer, Danny-boy. But yes—thirty-eight years is a long time to suffer. This man had likely given up hope. He had no one to help him into the water. And yet, on one particular day, Jesus saw him."

****

Grandpa Joe's voice softened as he read on:

"When Jesus saw him lying there and learned that he had been in this condition for a long time, He asked him, 'Do you want to get well?'"

Danny frowned. "Why would Jesus ask that? Of course he wanted to get well."

Grandpa Joe closed his Bible and rested it on his knee. "That's a good question, Danny. You see, Jesus wasn't just asking about his physical body—He was asking about his heart. Sometimes, when we've been broken for so long, we lose hope. We get comfortable in our suffering, and we stop believing that things can change. Jesus was asking, 'Are you ready to let Me change your life?'"

Hannah's voice was soft. "What did the man say?"

Grandpa opened the Bible again and read:

"'Sir,' the invalid replied, 'I have no one to help me into the pool when the water is stirred. While I am trying to get in, someone else goes down ahead of me.'"

Grandpa paused, looking out over the ruins of the pool. "This man felt alone, forgotten. But Jesus was about to show him—and all of us—that God never forgets the brokenhearted."

He continued: "Then Jesus said to him, 'Get up! Pick up your mat and walk.' At once the man was cured; he picked up his mat and walked."

****

The sunlight poured down, warming the stones beneath their feet as Grandpa closed his Bible.

"Do you see what happened here?" he asked gently. "The man didn't need the pool. He didn't need the water to be stirred. What he needed was Jesus. With just a word, Jesus healed him—no waiting, no conditions, just the power of God at work."

Danny stared down at the ruins of the pool. "So, Jesus didn't even touch him?"

"No, Danny," Grandpa said, shaking his head. "He simply spoke, and the man was healed. That's the authority of Jesus. When He says something, it happens."

Hannah looked up, her voice thoughtful. "Why did Jesus pick him, Grandpa? Out of all the people there, why him?"

Grandpa Joe's eyes softened. "That's one of the beautiful mysteries of God's grace, Hannah. Jesus saw this man in his pain, in his loneliness, and He chose to meet him there. God's love reaches out to us even when we feel forgotten, even when we've given up hope. And what Jesus did for this man, He still does for us today. He sees us in our brokenness, and He says, 'Get up.'"

****

They sat in silence for a moment, the story settling into their hearts. Danny picked up a small pebble and tossed it into a dry corner of the pool. "What happened to the man after he got healed?"

Grandpa smiled, flipping to the next verse. "Later, Jesus found him in the temple and said, *'See, you are well again. Stop sinning or something worse may happen to you.'*"

Danny's brow furrowed. "Worse? What could be worse than being paralyzed for thirty-eight years?"

Grandpa Joe placed a hand on Danny's shoulder. "Jesus was talking about something much deeper than the man's body. Physical healing is wonderful, but our souls need healing, too. Sin separates us from God. Jesus didn't just want the man to walk again—He wanted him to know the fullness of God's love, grace, and forgiveness."

****

The three of them stood, the quiet ruins of Bethesda stretching before them. Grandpa Joe's voice grew steady and clear, full of the warmth and authority that had guided their journey so far.

"Children, the Pool of Bethesda reminds us of this: we can't heal ourselves. We can't fix our brokenness on our own. But Jesus sees us, even in the places where no one else does. And when He speaks, everything changes. He calls us to stand up, to walk, to leave behind what's holding us back, and to trust Him completely."

Hannah looked up at Grandpa. "So, we don't have to wait by the water, do we?"

"No, Hannah," Grandpa said with a smile. "We don't have to wait. Jesus is ready to meet us wherever we are, right now. All we have to do is respond to His voice."

****

As they walked away from the pool, Danny looked back one last time. The broken stones didn't seem empty anymore—they felt like a reminder, a promise.

"Grandpa," he said quietly, "I think I'd want to hear Jesus say that to me. 'Get up.'"

Grandpa Joe nodded, his face full of joy. "He says it to all of us, Danny-boy. No matter how broken we feel, He's calling us to stand, to trust Him, and to live the life He has for us."

And as the sun began to dip lower, the three of them walked through the quiet streets of Jerusalem, the words of Jesus echoing in their hearts:

"Get up! Pick up your mat and walk."

CHAPTER 13:
THE FEEDING OF
THE 5,000

The hillside stretched wide and green under the afternoon sun, rolling gently toward the Sea of Galilee in the distance. Wildflowers dotted the grass, swaying in the light breeze that carried the soft hum of birdsong. Danny and Hannah dropped their backpacks onto the ground and flopped down with a sigh of relief.

"Are we having lunch here?" Danny asked, stretching out his legs and brushing dust from his sneakers.

Grandpa Joe chuckled as he eased himself onto a nearby rock, his walking stick resting beside him. "Not quite yet, Danny-boy, but this is the perfect place to talk about one of the greatest meals in history."

Hannah sat up straight, her curiosity piqued. "The greatest meal? Here?"

Grandpa's eyes twinkled with joy. "Yes, Hannah. Right here, or somewhere very close. This hillside is where Jesus performed one of His most famous miracles—the feeding of the 5,000. And what He did that day teaches us something about God's incredible provision."

****

The three of them sat in the warm grass as Grandpa opened his Bible, its worn pages flapping gently in the breeze.

"Now," Grandpa began, "picture this: Jesus had been teaching all day, and a huge crowd had gathered to hear Him. I'm talking about thousands of people—5,000 men, and that's not even counting the women and children."

"Wow," Danny said, his eyes wide. "That's like a whole stadium full of people!"

"Exactly," Grandpa said, nodding. "And as the day wore on, the people got hungry. The disciples—Jesus' closest followers—came to Him and said, *'Send the crowds away so they can go to the villages and buy food for themselves.'*"

Hannah frowned. "That makes sense. What else could they do with so many people?"

Grandpa smiled knowingly. "That's what the disciples thought too, Hannah. But listen to what Jesus said: *'You give them something to eat.'*"

Danny sat up. "Wait, what? How could they do that?"

Grandpa chuckled. "That's exactly what they asked! They were overwhelmed. They looked around at the crowd and said, *'It would take more than half a year's wages to buy enough bread for everyone to have a bite!'*"

Hannah's face crinkled in confusion. "So... what happened?"

****

Grandpa picked up a small piece of bread from his bag, holding it up for the children to see. "This is where the story gets amazing. One of the disciples, Andrew, found a boy in the crowd who had brought his lunch: five small loaves of bread and two fish. That's all they had—just enough for one person, maybe two."

"That wouldn't feed anyone!" Danny said, shaking his head.

Grandpa smiled. "It didn't seem like much, did it? But in the hands of Jesus, little becomes more than enough. Jesus took the bread and the fish, gave thanks to God, and began to break it into pieces. Then He handed it to the disciples to give to the crowd."

Grandpa paused, his voice soft but full of wonder. "And do you know what happened? Everyone ate. Every single person. Not just a little bit—but as much as they wanted."

Danny's eyes widened. "How is that even possible?"

"Because Jesus isn't limited by what we see," Grandpa said firmly. "When we trust Him with what little we have, He can multiply it beyond anything we could imagine. The Bible says they gathered up the leftovers, and there were twelve baskets full of bread and fish—more than they started with!"

****

For a moment, they sat in silence, the story settling into their hearts. The breeze rippled through the tall grass, and Hannah looked out over the sea below. "Why did Jesus do that, Grandpa?" she asked softly. "Why feed all those people?"

Grandpa Joe leaned forward, his eyes kind. "Because God cares for His people, Hannah. Jesus didn't just see a crowd—He saw individual people, each one with their own needs, their own hunger. And He met them right where they were."

He paused, his voice deepening with conviction. "This miracle teaches us something powerful: God is our provider. He knows our needs, big and small. And when we bring Him what little we have—whether it's our time, our gifts, or our faith—He can multiply it to bless others and to bless us."

Danny looked down at the piece of bread in Grandpa's hand, his voice quiet. "So it's not about how much we have, is it?"

"No, Danny-boy," Grandpa replied with a smile. "It's about who we give it to. The little boy didn't have much, but he gave it to Jesus. And Jesus used it to feed thousands. That's what happens when we put what we have—no matter how small—into God's hands."

****

Hannah plucked a blade of grass and twirled it between her fingers. "But what if I don't feel like I have anything to give,

67

Grandpa?"

Grandpa Joe's voice was gentle. "Oh, Hannah, you have more than you realize. God has given each of us gifts—our time, our talents, and our hearts. Sometimes it feels like what we have is too small to matter, but when we give it to Jesus, He uses it in ways we can't even see."

Danny looked up, his face thoughtful. "So, even if I don't feel important, God can still use me?"

Grandpa Joe smiled broadly. "Yes, Danny. That's the message of the feeding of the 5,000. God can use anyone. The boy with his small lunch probably never thought he'd be part of a miracle that day, but because he trusted Jesus, he was. God uses small things —like loaves and fish—and small people—like you and me—to do great things for His Kingdom."

****

As the sun began to dip lower in the sky, casting the hillside in a soft golden light, Grandpa Joe stood and stretched. "Children, remember this: God is our provider. When we feel like we don't have enough, or when life feels overwhelming, we can trust Him. He will give us what we need, and often, He will use us to bless others in the process."

Danny stood and stuffed his hands into his pockets, looking back at the sea. "I think I get it, Grandpa. Even if I only have a little, I can give it to Jesus."

"That's all He asks, Danny," Grandpa replied warmly. "Bring Him what you have, and let Him do the rest."

Hannah grinned and grabbed her backpack. "Maybe next time, I'll pack extra snacks—just in case Jesus wants to multiply them."

Grandpa Joe laughed, his deep chuckle echoing across the hillside. "You never know, Hannah. You never know."

As they walked back down the path, the hillside seemed to glow with the memory of the miracle that had happened there so long ago. And in their hearts, Danny and Hannah carried the simple yet profound truth Grandpa had shared:

When we trust Jesus with what little we have, He can do far more than we could ever imagine.

And somewhere, on that quiet hillside, it felt as if the echoes of Jesus' words still lingered, reminding them that God's provision is always enough.

CHAPTER 14: THE GOOD SHEPHERD

The quiet valley stretched out before them, a soft green carpet rolling gently between the hills. Wildflowers dotted the grass, and the occasional bleat of sheep echoed through the stillness. The air smelled fresh, as if it had just rained, though the sky above was clear and bright. Danny and Hannah followed Grandpa Joe down a narrow dirt path, their footsteps muffled by the soft earth.

They had stopped in the shade of a lone olive tree, its branches stretching wide like welcoming arms. Across the valley, a shepherd slowly walked ahead of his flock, his staff in hand. The sheep followed closely, trusting his every step.

"Look at that," Grandpa Joe said, pointing with his walking stick. "You see that shepherd leading his sheep? That right there is one of the oldest and most beautiful pictures of God's love for us."

Danny squinted at the distant figure. "How does that show God's love?"

Grandpa smiled and sat down on a large stone, motioning for Danny and Hannah to sit next to him. "Because, Danny, God Himself is our Shepherd. In fact, Jesus called Himself the *Good Shepherd.* Let me tell you what He said."

****

Grandpa Joe opened his Bible, the worn pages rustling in the light breeze. He paused for a moment, then began to read from the Gospel of John:

"I am the Good Shepherd. The Good Shepherd lays down His life for the sheep. The hired hand is not the shepherd and does not own the sheep. So when he sees the wolf coming, he abandons the sheep and runs away. Then the wolf attacks the flock and scatters it. The man runs away because he is a hired hand and cares nothing for the sheep. But I am the Good Shepherd; I know My sheep and My sheep know Me—just as the Father knows Me and I know the Father—and I lay down My life for the sheep."

Grandpa Joe closed the Bible gently and looked at the children. "Do you hear that? Jesus said He is the *Good Shepherd.* He knows us, He cares for us, and He loves us so much that He was willing to lay down His life to save us."

****

Hannah leaned back against the tree trunk, her face thoughtful. "Why does He call us sheep, Grandpa? Aren't sheep kind of... dumb?"

Grandpa Joe chuckled, his deep voice echoing in the quiet valley. "You're not wrong, Hannah. Sheep aren't the smartest animals. They wander off, they get lost easily, and they can't defend themselves when danger comes. That's why they need a shepherd—someone to guide them, protect them, and care for them."

Danny frowned. "So, are we like that? Do we wander off?"

Grandpa nodded, his eyes kind but serious. "Yes, Danny. The Bible says, *'We all, like sheep, have gone astray.'* Each of us has wandered away from God at some point. We get distracted, we lose our way, or we try to go through life on our own. But just like a shepherd doesn't give up on his sheep, Jesus doesn't give up on us."

Hannah looked across the valley at the shepherd, who was now gently nudging a stray lamb back to the flock. "Is that why Jesus came? To bring us back?"

"Yes, Hannah," Grandpa said softly. "Jesus came to seek and

save the lost. When we stray, He comes after us. When we're in danger, He protects us. And when we're hurting, He carries us."

****

The shepherd in the valley paused for a moment and called out in a low, steady voice. The sheep looked up, as if recognizing the sound, and began to follow him again. Grandpa pointed toward the scene.

"Do you see that? The sheep know his voice, and they follow him because they trust him. Jesus said, *'My sheep listen to My voice; I know them, and they follow Me.'* When we listen to Jesus— when we follow Him—we can trust that He'll lead us where we need to go."

Danny picked up a small stick and drew circles in the dirt. "But what if we don't hear Him, Grandpa? What if we don't know where He's leading us?"

Grandpa placed a hand on Danny's shoulder, his voice calm and steady. "Oh, Danny-boy, Jesus is always speaking to us. Sometimes we just have to slow down and listen. He speaks through His Word, through prayer, and even through the quiet moments like this one. The closer we stay to Him, the easier it is to hear His voice."

Danny looked up, his brow furrowed. "And what if we're scared? Like… what if wolves come?"

Grandpa's eyes softened as he leaned forward. "Jesus doesn't promise that life will always be easy, Danny. But He promises to be with us. The hired hand runs away when trouble comes, but the Good Shepherd never leaves His sheep. He fights for us. He laid down His life for us. That's how much He loves us."

****

For a long moment, the three of them sat in silence, watching the shepherd and his sheep move slowly across the valley. Hannah finally broke the stillness.

"Grandpa, is that why people say we should trust Jesus with

our whole lives? Because He's like the shepherd?"

"Yes, Hannah," Grandpa Joe said, his voice filled with warmth. "The Good Shepherd knows what's best for His sheep. He leads them to green pastures. He finds them when they're lost. He protects them when danger comes. And just like those sheep trust their shepherd, we can trust Jesus to guide us, to protect us, and to never let us go."

Danny looked out at the hills, his face thoughtful. "So we don't have to be afraid, right? Because He's with us?"

Grandpa smiled broadly, his eyes twinkling. "That's exactly right, Danny. The Bible says, *'Even though I walk through the darkest valley, I will fear no evil, for You are with me; Your rod and Your staff, they comfort me.'* Jesus, the Good Shepherd, walks with us through the highs and the lows. We may not always see Him, but He's always there."

****

The sun dipped lower in the sky, casting long shadows across the valley. Grandpa Joe stood slowly, leaning on his walking stick, and looked out at the sheep grazing in the distance. "Remember this, children: Jesus knows you. He loves you. And He calls you by name. No matter how far you wander, no matter what you face, He will always come after you."

Danny and Hannah stood beside him, their eyes on the shepherd below. The scene felt timeless, as if the very land remembered the words Jesus had spoken so long ago.

"Grandpa," Danny said softly, "I want to follow the Good Shepherd."

Grandpa Joe smiled, his face full of joy. "Then listen to His voice, Danny-boy. Trust Him, follow Him, and let Him lead you. Because with Jesus, you'll never walk alone."

As they turned back toward the path, the valley seemed to glow in the fading light, a picture of peace and protection. The shepherd's voice echoed softly, and the sheep followed—safe, secure, and loved.

And as the three of them walked together, Grandpa Joe's voice carried on the breeze, a quiet prayer for his grandchildren:

"Lord, help us to hear Your voice, to follow Your leading, and to trust You always, for You are the Good Shepherd of our souls."

CHAPTER 15: THE TRANSFIGURATION

The climb up Mount Tabor was steep, the path winding through clusters of trees and shrubs. The air grew thinner the higher they climbed, and the sunlight filtering through the branches cast golden beams on the rocky trail. Danny wiped sweat from his brow, looking up at Grandpa Joe, who was steadily making his way up with his walking stick.

"Grandpa," Danny called out, his voice a mix of exhaustion and curiosity, "why did Jesus go up mountains so much? Couldn't He just stay on flat ground?"

Grandpa Joe turned back and smiled, pausing for a moment. "That's a good question, Danny-boy. Jesus often went to mountains to pray, to teach, or to meet with God. You see, mountains are quiet places, far above the noise of the world, where the heart can hear God more clearly. And on this mountain, something happened that revealed who Jesus truly is."

Hannah, close behind, tilted her head. "What happened here, Grandpa?"

Grandpa Joe's voice grew reverent as he pointed upward. "This is Mount Tabor, one of the places believed to be where Jesus was transfigured—where He was revealed in glory to His closest disciples. It was here that the veil between heaven and earth seemed to lift, and for a moment, the disciples saw Jesus for who He truly is: the Son of God in all His majesty."

****

When they finally reached the summit, the view took their breath away. The green hills stretched endlessly toward the horizon, bathed in light. The sky seemed bigger here, the clouds soft and white against the brilliant blue. Grandpa Joe set his walking stick aside and sat on a large stone, his eyes lifting toward the heavens.

"Sit with me, children," he said gently, patting the ground. "Let me tell you what happened here, so long ago."

Danny and Hannah sank to the ground, listening intently as Grandpa opened his Bible, the pages fluttering in the soft mountain breeze.

"Jesus took three of His disciples—Peter, James, and John—up a mountain to pray. While they were there, something incredible happened. The Bible says, *'As He was praying, the appearance of His face changed, and His clothes became as bright as a flash of lightning.'*"

Hannah gasped. "What do you mean 'bright as lightning'? Was He glowing?"

"Yes, Hannah," Grandpa Joe replied, his voice full of awe. "Jesus was transfigured. His face and His clothing shone with a glory that no earthly light could match. The disciples had walked with Jesus for a long time, but in that moment, they saw Him as He truly is—divine, holy, and radiant with the glory of God."

****

Grandpa Joe paused, letting the moment sink in. The children stared at him, wide-eyed.

"But that's not all," Grandpa continued. "Two figures appeared with Him—Moses and Elijah, standing beside Jesus, talking with Him."

Danny furrowed his brow. "Moses and Elijah? Aren't they... from way back in the Old Testament?"

"Yes," Grandpa said, nodding. "Moses represented the Law, and Elijah represented the Prophets. Together, they pointed to Jesus, the fulfillment of everything God had promised through the Scriptures. Their presence showed that Jesus wasn't just another prophet or teacher—He was the One they had been waiting for."

Hannah hugged her knees to her chest. "What did the disciples do? Were they scared?"

Grandpa chuckled softly. "Oh, they were terrified, Hannah. The Bible says that Peter—always quick to speak—blurted out, *'Master, it is good for us to be here. Let us put up three shelters—one for You, one for Moses, and one for Elijah.'* He didn't know what to say, but he knew something holy was happening."

Danny smiled faintly. "That sounds like Peter. He always says something."

Grandpa Joe's voice grew stronger as he read the next part: *"While he was speaking, a cloud appeared and covered them, and they were afraid as they entered the cloud. A voice came from the cloud, saying, 'This is My Son, whom I have chosen; listen to Him.'"*

Grandpa paused, his face lifted toward the sky as if he could still hear the echo of that voice. "That was the voice of God Himself, Danny and Hannah. He was declaring to the disciples— and to all of us—that Jesus is not just a man. He is the Son of God. And God said, *'Listen to Him.'*"

****

The wind stirred gently around them, as if carrying the weight of that sacred moment. Danny broke the silence, his voice quiet. "Why do you think God showed them that, Grandpa?"

Grandpa turned to face him, his expression tender but full of conviction. "Because the disciples needed to see the truth about Jesus. They had heard His teachings. They had seen His miracles. But now, God was showing them His glory—revealing that Jesus was not just a man sent by God, but God Himself in human form."

Hannah looked up, her voice soft. "Do you think Jesus wanted to show them so they wouldn't doubt?"

"Yes, Hannah," Grandpa said, nodding. "Jesus knew the road ahead would be hard. He knew He would go to the cross to die for our sins. The disciples needed to know beyond a shadow of a doubt who He was so that their faith could carry them through the darkest days. Seeing His glory on this mountain reminded them that Jesus is the light, even when everything around them seemed dark."

****

Danny glanced out at the horizon, the world spread out below them. "Do you think we'll ever see Jesus like that, Grandpa?"

Grandpa Joe's face broke into a smile, his voice full of hope. "Yes, Danny-boy, we will. One day, the Bible tells us that Jesus will return—not as a humble servant, but in all His glory as King of kings and Lord of lords. And every eye will see Him. But even now, when we put our faith in Him, we can see glimpses of His glory—through His Word, through His creation, and through the way He changes our hearts."

Hannah looked around the mountaintop, her voice quiet. "It feels like He's close here. Like we can hear Him."

Grandpa Joe nodded, his eyes soft. "That's the beauty of this place, Hannah. On the mountaintop, away from the noise and distractions, our hearts can hear God's voice more clearly. And just like God said to the disciples, He's still saying to us today: 'This is My Son. Listen to Him.'"

****

As they began their descent, the golden light of the setting sun bathed the mountaintop in a glow that seemed almost heavenly. The world below felt far away, but the truth of what Grandpa had shared lingered in their hearts.

"Grandpa," Danny said softly, "I think I want to listen to Jesus more."

Grandpa Joe smiled, his voice steady and full of joy. "That's the best thing you could ever do, Danny. When you listen to Him, you'll see His glory—not just on the mountaintops, but in your everyday life. And when you follow Him, He will lead you home."

Hannah reached for Grandpa's hand, holding it tightly as they walked. "I'm glad we came here, Grandpa."

"So am I, Hannah," Grandpa Joe said, glancing back up at the mountaintop one last time. "Because sometimes, we all need to be reminded of who Jesus is—and how His light shines, even when everything else fades."

And as they continued down the path, the mountain stood behind them, a silent witness to the glory of Christ—a glimpse of the King who reigns now and forever.

CHAPTER 16: JERICHO—THE BLIND MAN SEES

The sun beat down on the ancient city of Jericho, its golden light reflecting off the dusty stones and sunbaked streets. Palms swayed gently in the breeze, their shadows dancing on the walls of the city that had stood for thousands of years. Danny wiped the sweat from his brow as they walked along a narrow street, lined with old buildings and crumbling walls.

"Grandpa," Danny said, squinting against the glare, "Jericho feels different from Galilee. It's so… hot and dry."

Grandpa Joe smiled and tapped his walking stick rhythmically on the ground. "It is, Danny-boy, but Jericho has a history unlike any other. This is the city where the walls came tumbling down in the days of Joshua. And later, it was here that a blind man named Bartimaeus cried out to Jesus—and everything changed."

Hannah tilted her head, intrigued. "Bartimaeus? I've never heard of him."

"Well," Grandpa said, his voice warm and steady, "you're about to. His story teaches us about faith—faith that won't give up, no matter what stands in the way."

****

They stopped in the shade of a large stone arch, a welcome relief from the heat. Grandpa Joe motioned for them to sit on a low stone wall as he opened his Bible. He leaned forward, his eyes twinkling with purpose, as he began to tell the story.

"Now listen carefully, children. Jesus was on His way to Jerusalem, and He passed through Jericho. By this time, crowds were everywhere. People had heard about His miracles—how He healed the sick, fed the hungry, and even raised the dead. So when Jesus came near, people gathered along the road, hoping to see Him."

Danny nodded. "It must have been loud, huh? Lots of people shouting and pushing."

Grandpa smiled. "It was. And sitting on the side of the road that day was a blind man named Bartimaeus. He couldn't see the crowds, but he could hear them. He heard that Jesus of Nazareth was passing by, and in his heart, Bartimaeus knew that this was his chance—his only chance—to be healed."

****

Grandpa's voice grew stronger, filled with conviction as he read from the Gospel of Mark:

"When he heard that it was Jesus of Nazareth, he began to shout, 'Jesus, Son of David, have mercy on me!'"

Hannah looked up quickly. "Did people help him?"

Grandpa Joe shook his head. "No, Hannah. In fact, the people told him to be quiet. They tried to silence him, probably thinking he was just a nuisance—someone who didn't matter. But do you know what Bartimaeus did?"

Danny's brow furrowed. "What?"

Grandpa's voice rang out with power, as if he could hear Bartimaeus calling even now. "He shouted *even louder!* '*Son of David, have mercy on me!*' Bartimaeus didn't care what anyone thought. He wasn't going to let the crowd stop him. His faith was persistent—he believed that Jesus could help him, and nothing would keep him from asking."

Hannah's eyes widened. "What did Jesus do?"

****

Grandpa Joe smiled and read on:

"Jesus stopped and said, 'Call him.' So they called to the blind man, 'Cheer up! On your feet! He's calling you.' Throwing his cloak aside, he jumped to his feet and came to Jesus."

Grandpa paused, looking at Danny and Hannah. "Now think about that. Jesus—surrounded by noise and crowds—*stopped*. He heard Bartimaeus' cry. He noticed the man that everyone else overlooked. And He called him to come."

Danny sat up straighter. "And then what happened?"

Grandpa's voice softened, filled with reverence. "Jesus asked him a simple question: *'What do you want Me to do for you?'* And Bartimaeus said, *'Rabbi, I want to see.'*"

Hannah whispered, "Did Jesus heal him?"

"Oh, yes," Grandpa Joe said, nodding with a smile. "Jesus said to him, *'Go, your faith has healed you.'* And immediately, Bartimaeus received his sight. He could see! But do you know what he did next?"

Danny shrugged. "Went home?"

"No, Danny-boy," Grandpa said with a grin. "The Bible says Bartimaeus followed Jesus along the road. He didn't just receive his sight and go his own way—he used his new life to follow the One who had healed him."

****

The three of them sat quietly for a moment, the story sinking in. The heat of Jericho felt far away as the children imagined Bartimaeus standing before Jesus, his face full of wonder as the world came into view for the first time.

"Why did Jesus ask him what he wanted?" Hannah asked softly. "Didn't He already know?"

Grandpa Joe nodded thoughtfully. "He did know, Hannah. Jesus knows our needs before we even ask. But He wants us to come to Him in faith, to ask, to trust Him. When Bartimaeus said, *'Rabbi, I want to see,'* it wasn't just his eyes that were opened —it was his heart. Jesus saw his faith, and that's what made the difference."

****

Danny looked down, his voice quiet. "Do you think Jesus hears us when we call out, like Bartimaeus?"

Grandpa's voice was firm and clear, like a steady beacon of hope. "Oh, yes, Danny. Jesus always hears us. You see, Bartimaeus didn't let the crowd stop him. He didn't let his doubts keep him quiet. He cried out to Jesus with all the faith he had. And when we cry out to Him—when we come to Him with our struggles, our fears, or our needs—He hears us, and He answers."

Danny picked up a small stone and tossed it gently into the dust. "Even if we feel small or forgotten?"

Grandpa Joe's face softened. "Especially then, Danny. Jesus specializes in seeing the people the world overlooks. The blind, the brokenhearted, the ones who feel invisible—He calls them to Himself and says, 'What do you want Me to do for you?' Because in His eyes, every single person matters."

****

Hannah leaned her head against Grandpa's shoulder. "I think I'd like to be like Bartimaeus—someone who doesn't give up."

Grandpa smiled, resting his hand gently on her head. "That's a good prayer, Hannah. God loves persistent faith—the kind of faith that doesn't stop calling out to Him, no matter what. Because when we trust Him with all our hearts, He does far more than we could ever imagine."

****

The sun dipped lower in the sky as they began to walk back through the quiet streets of Jericho. Danny looked up at Grandpa, his voice steady. "I think I'll start calling out to Jesus more, Grandpa. Like Bartimaeus did."

Grandpa Joe smiled, his heart full. "That's the best decision you can make, Danny-boy. Call out to Him, trust Him, and follow Him. Because just like Bartimaeus, when we encounter Jesus, our lives are never the same."

As they made their way back toward the edge of the city, the stones of Jericho seemed to glow in the golden light. Danny and Hannah's hearts were full of something new—a confidence that Jesus not only heard them, but He saw them, just like He saw Bartimaeus.

And somewhere deep within, they understood that no cry of faith ever goes unanswered.

CHAPTER 17: THE ROAD TO JERUSALEM

The road stretched out before them, dusty and winding, as it climbed toward the holy city of Jerusalem. The air carried a sense of anticipation, as if even the stones beneath their feet knew they were approaching something sacred. The distant outline of Jerusalem's walls rose like a shadow against the brilliant blue sky, its ancient gates waiting silently.

Grandpa Joe walked slowly, his steady steps marked by the tap of his walking stick on the rocky path. Danny and Hannah followed close behind, their shoes kicking up small clouds of dust as they moved. There was something different about Grandpa Joe's demeanor today—he was quieter, more reflective, as if the weight of the place and its history rested on his shoulders.

"Grandpa," Danny said finally, breaking the silence, "why does it feel so serious here?"

Grandpa paused, leaning on his stick as he turned to face them. His face was lined with thought, his eyes looking toward the city ahead. "Because, Danny-boy, this road we're on is the same road Jesus traveled. It's the road to Jerusalem—the road to His final days on Earth."

****

They sat on a low stone wall at the edge of the path, looking out at the hills that framed the horizon. Grandpa Joe set his Bible on his knee and let the silence linger for a moment, gathering his thoughts.

"Children," he began, his voice steady and low, "this road represents more than just a journey—it's a turning point. For three years, Jesus had traveled through Galilee and Judea. He healed the sick, fed the hungry, and brought hope to the brokenhearted. He taught with authority, telling people about God's Kingdom and inviting them to follow Him. But everything He did led Him here—to Jerusalem."

Hannah looked up at Grandpa, her brow furrowed. "Why did He have to go to Jerusalem?"

Grandpa smiled faintly, his eyes full of understanding. "Because that's where His mission would be completed, Hannah. Jesus knew what waited for Him in Jerusalem: rejection, suffering, and death. But He went anyway, because He loved us. He went for you. He went for me."

Danny looked down at the ground, his voice small. "Didn't He… didn't He know how hard it would be?"

"Oh, He knew, Danny," Grandpa said softly. "The Bible tells us that Jesus told His disciples exactly what would happen. He said, *'We are going up to Jerusalem, and the Son of Man will be delivered over to the chief priests and the teachers of the law. They will condemn Him to death and hand Him over to the Gentiles, who will mock Him and spit on Him, flog Him and kill Him. Three days later He will rise.'*"

Grandpa paused, letting the words sink in, his voice filled with awe. "He knew it all—the betrayal, the pain, the cross. And yet He went willingly, because He knew it was the only way to save us from our sin."

****

The wind stirred the air, as if whispering the weight of what Grandpa Joe had just said. Danny looked up, his face troubled. "Why would He do that? Why would He go through all that for us?"

Grandpa's voice was tender, yet strong. "Because He loves us,

Danny. The Bible says, *'Greater love has no one than this: to lay down one's life for one's friends.'* Jesus loved us so much that He chose the road to Jerusalem. He chose the cross. He chose to bear the weight of our sin so that we could be forgiven."

Hannah hugged her knees to her chest. "Didn't His disciples try to stop Him?"

Grandpa nodded, a bittersweet smile on his lips. "They did, Hannah. Peter even said, *'Never, Lord! This shall never happen to You!'* But Jesus told Peter that it had to happen. He knew the road to the cross was the reason He had come. He wasn't just a teacher or a healer—He was the Lamb of God, come to take away the sin of the world."

****

For a moment, they sat in silence, the gravity of Grandpa Joe's words pressing on their hearts. The road ahead felt more than just a path—it felt like a sacred thread woven into the greatest story ever told.

Danny finally spoke, his voice hesitant. "Was He afraid, Grandpa?"

Grandpa Joe's gaze softened, and he looked out toward Jerusalem. "Yes, Danny. In His humanity, Jesus felt every bit of the weight of what was coming. The Bible tells us that, in the Garden of Gethsemane, He prayed, *'Father, if You are willing, take this cup from Me; yet not My will, but Yours be done.'* He was sorrowful, even to the point of anguish. But in His love and obedience, He chose the cross anyway. That's what makes His sacrifice so powerful."

Danny's face was serious now, as if something had settled deep in his heart. "I don't think I've ever heard it like that before. Like… He chose it because He loves us."

Grandpa Joe smiled, resting a hand on Danny's shoulder. "That's exactly right, Danny-boy. Jesus walked this road for us. And every step He took was filled with love—love for you, love for Hannah, love for every single person in this world."

****

The three of them stood and began walking again, the city of Jerusalem growing larger in the distance. Grandpa Joe's voice rose gently as they walked, his words carrying the weight of truth and grace.

"Children, I want you to remember this: the road to Jerusalem reminds us of the price Jesus paid for our salvation. It wasn't easy. It wasn't comfortable. But it was necessary. And because of what He did—because He laid down His life—we can be forgiven. We can know God. And we can have the promise of eternal life."

Hannah looked up at Grandpa, her eyes wide. "So, we're walking where Jesus walked?"

"Yes, Hannah," Grandpa said, his voice soft but steady. "And every step reminds us that His journey wasn't just for long ago— it was for us, right here, right now. The same Jesus who walked this road to Jerusalem is still calling us to follow Him today."

****

As they reached a ridge overlooking the city, Grandpa Joe stopped and turned to face the children. Jerusalem lay below them, its ancient walls glowing golden in the afternoon light.

"Look at that city," Grandpa said, his voice quiet with reverence. "It was here that Jesus showed the world what true love looks like. He came as the King of kings, but not to rule with power or armies. He came to lay down His life so that we could be saved."

Danny stared at the city, his voice almost a whisper. "What should we do, Grandpa?"

Grandpa Joe smiled, his eyes glistening. "Follow Him, Danny. Trust Him. Jesus walked this road for you, and now He invites you to walk with Him. He said, *'Whoever wants to be My disciple must deny themselves and take up their cross daily and follow Me.'* The road may not always be easy, but it's the road that leads to life."

****

The wind blew softly across the hilltop as they stood together, looking out at Jerusalem. Danny and Hannah felt something new stirring in their hearts—a deeper understanding of Jesus' love and sacrifice.

Grandpa Joe's voice, steady and full of hope, echoed one last time:

"The road to Jerusalem was a road of suffering, but it was also a road of victory. Because of Jesus, the story doesn't end with the cross—it ends with an empty tomb and a risen Savior. And that, children, is the greatest news the world has ever heard."

As they began the walk down the hill, the city ahead seemed brighter, as if the light of Jesus' love still rested over its walls. And in their hearts, they carried the weight and wonder of the road He chose—for them, and for the world.

CHAPTER 18: PALM SUNDAY IN JERUSALEM

The narrow, winding road descended from the Mount of Olives into the bustling city of Jerusalem. The stones underfoot, worn smooth by centuries of footsteps, seemed to whisper stories of those who had traveled this path long ago. Olive trees lined the hillside, their silvery leaves shimmering in the gentle breeze. From here, the city of Jerusalem stretched before them, its ancient walls glowing golden in the morning sunlight.

Danny and Hannah walked quietly beside Grandpa Joe, who moved slowly but purposefully, his walking stick tapping rhythmically on the ground. There was a sense of something sacred in the air, as if the very road they were walking held its breath, remembering what had happened here.

"Grandpa," Hannah said softly, breaking the stillness, "is this really the path Jesus took?"

Grandpa Joe paused, looking out over the city below. "Yes, Hannah. This is the Palm Sunday road—the road Jesus traveled when He entered Jerusalem for the final time. The Bible calls it His *Triumphal Entry.* The people welcomed Him as their King that day, though many didn't fully understand who He was or why He had come."

****

They found a quiet place along the path and sat on a low stone wall under the shade of an olive tree. Grandpa Joe took a deep breath, his eyes bright with the joy of the story he was about to share.

"Children," he began, "I want you to imagine it. The city was alive with excitement. Crowds had gathered in Jerusalem for the Passover, the great feast celebrating how God had delivered His people from Egypt. But this Passover would be like no other—because Jesus was coming."

Danny leaned forward, his eyes wide. "Did everyone know who He was?"

Grandpa shook his head. "Not everyone, Danny. But word had spread about Him. People had heard how He healed the sick, fed the multitudes, and even raised the dead. They were beginning to believe that maybe—just maybe—Jesus was the Messiah, the Savior they had been waiting for."

He opened his Bible and began to read:

"As Jesus approached Bethphage and Bethany at the hill called the Mount of Olives, He sent two of His disciples, saying to them, 'Go to the village ahead of you, and as you enter it, you will find a colt tied there, which no one has ever ridden. Untie it and bring it here.'"

Hannah tilted her head. "Why a colt? Couldn't Jesus have ridden something more... majestic?"

Grandpa Joe smiled gently. "That's a good question, Hannah. Kings often rode warhorses when they came in power, but Jesus chose a humble colt because He came not as a warrior king, but as the Prince of Peace. The prophet Zechariah had foretold this hundreds of years earlier, saying, *'See, your king comes to you, righteous and victorious, lowly and riding on a donkey.'* Jesus fulfilled that prophecy perfectly."

****

Grandpa Joe's voice grew stronger as he continued. "When the disciples brought the colt to Jesus, they threw their cloaks over its back, and Jesus sat on it. As He rode down this very road, the people began to gather. They spread their cloaks on the ground like a royal carpet, and they waved palm branches, shouting with joy."

Danny looked up, his brow furrowed. "Why palm branches, Grandpa?"

"Palm branches were a symbol of victory, Danny," Grandpa explained. "The people were celebrating Jesus as their King, their Deliverer. They shouted, *'Hosanna! Blessed is He who comes in the name of the Lord!'* 'Hosanna' means 'Save us now!' They believed Jesus was coming to set them free from the Romans and restore their kingdom."

Hannah looked out at the path, imagining the scene. "That sounds like a parade!"

Grandpa nodded, his voice warm. "Yes, Hannah. It was like a royal procession. But here's the thing: Jesus wasn't coming to Jerusalem to claim an earthly throne. His kingdom was not of this world. He came to save the people not from the Romans, but from something far greater—from sin and death itself."

****

Danny's voice grew quieter. "Did the people know that, Grandpa?"

Grandpa Joe shook his head sadly. "No, Danny. Many of them didn't understand. They were looking for a king of power and armies, not a humble Savior who would lay down His life for them. And some of the same people who shouted 'Hosanna!' on Palm Sunday would shout 'Crucify Him!' just days later."

Hannah looked up sharply. "Why? Why would they turn on Him?"

Grandpa's face softened with both sorrow and awe. "Because Jesus didn't meet their expectations. They wanted a Messiah who would conquer their enemies, but Jesus came to conquer sin. They didn't see that His greatest victory would come through the cross."

He paused and looked at the children, his voice steady and full of hope. "But make no mistake—Jesus knew what He was doing. He knew that this road would lead to His suffering and death, and yet He came willingly. He rode into Jerusalem with full knowledge of what awaited Him, because His love for us is that great."

****

The wind stirred gently through the olive trees, carrying the quiet weight of Grandpa Joe's words. Danny stared at the path ahead, as if seeing the crowd, the palm branches, and the figure of Jesus riding in peace.

"Grandpa," Danny said softly, "if Jesus knew they would turn on Him, why did He still go?"

Grandpa placed his hand on Danny's shoulder, his voice strong but tender. "Because, Danny, Jesus came to save us. He didn't come to be served, but to serve—and to give His life as a ransom for many. The Bible says, *'For God so loved the world that He gave His one and only Son, that whoever believes in Him shall not perish but have eternal life.'* Jesus loved us enough to walk this road— knowing it would lead to the cross—so that we could have life forever with Him."

****

Hannah looked down at the palm leaves that had fallen from the nearby trees. "So Palm Sunday is like the beginning of the end, isn't it?"

Grandpa smiled gently. "In one sense, yes, Hannah. Palm Sunday begins the final days of Jesus' life on Earth. But in another sense, it's the beginning of something far greater—the road to our salvation. Jesus came as a humble King that day, but when He returns, He will come in all His glory as the King of kings and Lord of lords."

Danny looked up, a spark of understanding in his eyes. "So, He's not done yet."

Grandpa Joe's face broke into a smile, his voice strong with joy. "That's right, Danny-boy. The story isn't over. Palm Sunday reminds us that Jesus is our King—not just back then, but now and forever. And when we shout 'Hosanna,' we're still crying out, 'Save us now, Lord!' Because He is the only One who can."

****

As they stood and began walking down the Palm Sunday road, Danny and Hannah were quiet, lost in thought. The city of Jerusalem rose before them, just as it had for Jesus so many years ago.

Grandpa Joe's voice carried on the wind, his words full of reverence. "Children, remember this: Jesus is the King who chose humility, who chose sacrifice, and who chose us. He came to save us—not with swords or armies, but with His love. And because of what He did, we can follow Him, knowing that the victory has already been won."

The road stretched on, but in their hearts, Danny and Hannah could see it clearly: the palm branches waving, the voices shouting, and Jesus, the humble King, riding toward His destiny.

And as they walked, they whispered the words for themselves—words of hope, of faith, and of praise:

"Hosanna! Blessed is He who comes in the name of the Lord."

CHAPTER 19: THE TEMPLE COURTYARD

The ruins of the Temple courtyard stood solemn and silent, their stones weathered by time. Though much of it had crumbled, the outline of the massive space still whispered of its former grandeur—a place once filled with worshipers, priests, and pilgrims from far and wide. Now, sunlight streamed through broken arches, casting long shadows across the stone-paved ground.

Danny and Hannah followed Grandpa Joe through the courtyard, their footsteps echoing softly. Birds flitted above, their wings brushing the still air, as if even they understood the weight of this place. Grandpa Joe paused in the center of the courtyard, leaning on his walking stick, his gaze distant and thoughtful.

"Grandpa," Danny said, looking around, "is this where people worshipped God?"

"Yes, Danny-boy," Grandpa replied, his voice quiet but strong. "This is what remains of the Temple—the place that once stood as the very heart of Jerusalem, the house of God. It was a place of prayer, sacrifice, and worship. But during Jesus' time, something happened here that broke His heart—and stirred His righteous anger."

****

They sat on a stone ledge at the edge of the courtyard as Grandpa Joe opened his Bible, the gentle breeze lifting the worn pages. He paused for a moment before speaking, his voice filled with reverence and purpose.

"Children, this Temple was sacred. It was built to honor God, a place where people could come to seek Him, to pray, and to draw near to His presence. But when Jesus entered the Temple courtyard one day, He found something that didn't belong."

"What did He find, Grandpa?" Hannah asked, her eyes wide with curiosity.

Grandpa Joe leaned forward, his gaze intense. "Instead of worship and prayer, Jesus found merchants and money changers filling the Temple courts. They were selling animals for sacrifices and exchanging money—turning God's house into a marketplace."

Danny frowned. "But didn't people need animals for sacrifices? What was so bad about that?"

Grandpa Joe nodded gently. "You're right, Danny. People came from all over, and they needed animals to offer sacrifices. But the merchants were doing more than providing a service— they were cheating people. They overcharged for animals and inflated prices for exchanging coins, taking advantage of those who came to worship."

Hannah's brow furrowed. "That's not fair. And it doesn't sound very holy."

Grandpa's voice grew firm, filled with a quiet authority. "It wasn't, Hannah. And Jesus knew it. When He entered the courtyard that day, He saw the greed, the injustice, and the way God's house was being dishonored. And He acted."

****

Grandpa Joe opened his Bible and began to read, his voice ringing clear and steady:

"Jesus entered the Temple courts and drove out all who were buying and selling there. He overturned the tables of the money changers and the benches of those selling doves. 'It is written,' He said to them, 'My house will be called a house of prayer, but you are making it 'a

den of robbers.'"

Hannah gasped. "He overturned their tables? Jesus got angry?"

Grandpa Joe nodded, his voice calm but firm. "Yes, Hannah. But it wasn't the kind of anger we often think of. This was *righteous* anger—holy and just. Jesus wasn't angry out of selfishness. He was angry because God's house, a place meant for prayer and worship, had been corrupted. People were being robbed, and the holiness of God's presence was being treated with disrespect."

Danny looked up. "So it was like Jesus was defending God's house?"

"Exactly, Danny," Grandpa said, his eyes shining with conviction. "Jesus wasn't just defending the Temple; He was defending what the Temple represented—a place where people could meet God. He cared deeply about that because He knew how much we need to come to God in prayer. The Bible says, *'Zeal for Your house will consume Me.'* Jesus' heart burned with passion for His Father's house and for people to worship in spirit and in truth."

****

For a moment, they sat quietly, the weight of the story settling on them. The Temple ruins around them seemed to echo with the memory of Jesus' righteous footsteps, the clatter of tables being overturned, and the sound of His words: *"My house will be called a house of prayer."*

"Grandpa," Hannah said softly, "why does God care so much about prayer?"

Grandpa's face softened, his voice gentle. "Because, Hannah, prayer is how we talk to God. It's how we come close to Him, sharing our hearts and listening for His voice. The Temple was supposed to be a place where people could come and know they were near God—where they could pray, confess their sins, and seek His presence."

Danny kicked a small stone, his voice thoughtful. "But we don't have a Temple anymore. Where do we pray now?"

Grandpa Joe smiled warmly. "That's a wonderful question, Danny-boy. Jesus changed everything. When He came, He became the perfect sacrifice for our sins. Because of Him, we don't need to go to a physical Temple to meet with God. The Bible tells us that now, our hearts are God's temple. When we put our faith in Jesus, His Spirit lives within us, and we can pray to Him anytime, anywhere."

****

Hannah looked out at the ruins, her voice soft. "So, Jesus cared about the Temple because He cares about our hearts?"

Grandpa nodded, his eyes bright with joy. "That's exactly right, Hannah. Just as Jesus cleansed the Temple that day, He wants to cleanse our hearts too. Sometimes, things like sin, selfishness, or distractions crowd into our lives, just like the merchants in the Temple. But Jesus, in His love, calls us to turn back to Him. He wants our hearts to be places of worship, prayer, and holiness."

Danny looked up at Grandpa, a flicker of understanding on his face. "So when we pray, we're like the people in the Temple—coming close to God?"

Grandpa Joe smiled, placing a hand on Danny's shoulder. "Yes, Danny. Prayer isn't just talking to the air; it's coming into the presence of a holy and loving God who hears us. Jesus said, *'My house will be called a house of prayer for all nations.'* That invitation is for everyone—young and old, near and far. And through Jesus, we can boldly come to God with all our hearts."

****

The afternoon sun dipped lower in the sky, casting golden light across the courtyard. Grandpa Joe stood and looked out over the ruins, his voice strong and clear.

"Children, let's never forget what Jesus taught us here: God's house—and our hearts—are meant to be places of worship, not distraction. When we come to Him in prayer, we honor Him.

And when we allow Him to cleanse our hearts, we make room for His Spirit to live and work in us."

Danny and Hannah stood with him, their eyes following his gaze over the quiet stones. Danny's voice broke the stillness. "Grandpa, I think I want my heart to be like that—a place where God is welcome."

Grandpa Joe smiled, his face filled with joy. "That's a prayer God always answers, Danny-boy. When we invite Jesus into our hearts, He doesn't just come to visit—He makes His home there, forever."

****

As they left the Temple courtyard, the wind stirred softly through the ruins, as if carrying the echoes of Jesus' words:

"My house will be called a house of prayer."

And in their hearts, Danny and Hannah carried a new understanding—that Jesus, the One who overturned the tables, still calls us to let Him cleanse, restore, and dwell within us.

CHAPTER 20:
LESSONS FROM
A WIDOW

The afternoon sun hung low over the ancient city of Jerusalem, bathing the Temple Mount in a warm golden light. Danny and Hannah followed Grandpa Joe up a set of stone steps, their shoes tapping against the timeworn stones. The crowds had thinned out, leaving the temple ruins quieter than they had been earlier in the day.

"Where are we going now, Grandpa?" Danny asked, shielding his eyes from the sun.

Grandpa Joe smiled softly, resting on his walking stick for a moment. "We're going to the place where Jesus taught one of His most powerful lessons—one that had nothing to do with how much someone had, but everything to do with the heart behind what they gave."

"What kind of lesson?" Hannah asked, curious.

Grandpa motioned them to follow him as they reached a small area that once served as part of the Temple treasury. He pointed to a series of stone chests where people would have once placed their offerings.

"This is where Jesus sat and watched people give their gifts," Grandpa said gently. "And it's where He noticed someone no one else saw—a poor widow who gave more than anyone could have imagined."

****

The three of them sat on a low wall nearby, the Temple ruins stretching around them. Grandpa Joe opened his Bible and paused, as if he could see the story unfolding before him.

"Children," he began, "this story is found in the Gospel of Mark. The Bible says that Jesus sat down opposite the place where the offerings were put and watched the crowd placing their money into the Temple treasury. Many rich people came by and gave large sums of money—gifts that impressed the people watching."

Danny leaned forward. "Did Jesus say anything about them?"

Grandpa Joe shook his head. "No, Danny-boy. He saw what they gave, but He didn't focus on them. Instead, He noticed someone the crowd overlooked—a poor widow."

He opened his Bible and read in a steady, clear voice:

"But a poor widow came and put in two very small copper coins, worth only a few cents. Calling His disciples to Him, Jesus said, 'Truly I tell you, this poor widow has put more into the treasury than all the others. They all gave out of their wealth; but she, out of her poverty, put in everything—all she had to live on.'"

****

Hannah tilted her head, her brow furrowed. "Two small coins? How could that be more than what the rich people gave?"

Grandpa Joe's eyes softened, and he smiled. "Because, Hannah, Jesus wasn't looking at the size of the gift—He was looking at the heart behind it. The rich gave out of their abundance. They had plenty left over. But the widow... she gave everything she had. Her gift was small in the world's eyes, but it was priceless to God because it came from a heart of trust, sacrifice, and love."

Danny picked up a pebble and turned it over in his hand. "But why would she give everything, Grandpa? Didn't she need it to live?"

Grandpa Joe nodded. "That's what makes her gift so beautiful,

Danny. She trusted God completely. By giving her last coins, she was saying, 'Lord, I trust You to provide for me.' Her faith was stronger than her fear of having nothing."

****

For a moment, the three of them sat quietly, as if the wind itself carried the story. Grandpa Joe continued, his voice deep and steady.

"This widow teaches us a powerful lesson about sacrificial giving. You see, it's not just about money—it's about the heart. When we give, whether it's our time, our talents, or our resources, God isn't looking at how much we give; He's looking at how much it costs us."

Hannah looked up, her voice soft. "What do you mean, Grandpa?"

"I mean," Grandpa said gently, "that real giving—giving that pleases God—often requires sacrifice. It's easy to give when we have plenty. But when we give something that costs us—something we feel we can't afford to lose—that's when we show the depth of our trust in God."

Danny frowned slightly. "So... does God want us to give everything?"

Grandpa smiled and placed a hand on Danny's shoulder. "Danny-boy, God doesn't measure our giving the way the world does. He doesn't ask for everything we own, but He does ask for our hearts. When we give to Him—whether it's through our time, our love, or what we have—we're saying, 'Lord, I trust You. I believe You are enough for me.' That's the kind of faith this widow had."

****

Hannah hugged her knees to her chest. "But what if we don't have much to give, Grandpa? Does it still matter?"

Grandpa Joe's voice grew firm, yet full of kindness. "Oh yes, Hannah. That's the beauty of this story. It's not about how much we have—it's about giving with a willing heart. The widow's offering was tiny in the eyes of others, but to God, it was precious. Jesus saw her faith, and He honored it."

He looked at both of them, his eyes glistening. "Never think you're too small to make a difference. God can take even the smallest gift and use it in ways we can't imagine. When we give with a heart of love and trust, God multiplies it."

****

The wind stirred gently, rustling the pages of Grandpa Joe's Bible as he closed it and set it aside. Danny and Hannah looked out at the ruins of the Temple treasury, imagining the poor widow stepping forward to give her coins, unnoticed by everyone but Jesus.

"Grandpa," Danny said after a moment, "I think the widow must have been really brave."

Grandpa smiled, his face full of joy. "She was, Danny. Her faith gave her courage. She didn't give because she was rich—she gave because she knew her true treasure was in God's hands. And that's what Jesus invites us to do, too. When we trust Him with what we have, He promises to care for us."

Hannah looked thoughtful. "So, it's like we're giving back to God because He's given us so much already?"

Grandpa nodded. "That's exactly right, Hannah. Everything we have comes from God. When we give, we're simply giving back to Him out of gratitude. And when we give sacrificially—like the widow did—we show our faith in His goodness and provision."

****

As they stood and began to walk back, Grandpa Joe looked at the children with a quiet smile. "Children, the widow's two coins remind us of this: God doesn't ask for much, but He asks for our best. He asks for our trust, our love, and our willingness to give. When we do that, no gift is ever too small for Him to use."

Danny's voice broke the silence as they walked. "Grandpa, I think I want to give more—like the widow did."

Grandpa Joe rested a hand on his shoulder, his heart full. "That's the best kind of gift, Danny-boy—one that comes from a willing and trusting heart. Remember, God can take what seems small and turn it into something extraordinary."

Hannah looked up at Grandpa as they neared the edge of the courtyard. "Grandpa, I think Jesus really loved that widow."

Grandpa Joe smiled, his eyes soft with warmth. "He did, Hannah. And He loves us the same way—because He looks at our hearts."

****

The sun dipped lower in the sky, casting long shadows across the temple ruins. As they walked together, Grandpa Joe's voice carried one last truth through the quiet air:

"Children, let's never forget what Jesus taught us here: True giving isn't measured by the size of the gift—it's measured by the size of the sacrifice, the trust, and the love behind it. And no matter how small our offering may seem, when we give it to God, it becomes something beautiful in His hands."

And as the ancient stones seemed to reflect the weight of those words, Danny and Hannah walked away with a new understanding of what it meant to give—not just what they had, but who they were—back to God.

PART 3: THE PASSION OF JESUS

CHAPTER 21: THE LAST SUPPER ROOM

The Upper Room was simple but sacred, its stone walls and wooden beams holding memories that stretched back two thousand years. Though quiet now, the air seemed to carry the faint echoes of that night—Jesus' final hours with His disciples before He would face the cross. Sunlight streamed through a small window, falling on the stone floor where countless feet had once stood.

Danny and Hannah followed Grandpa Joe into the room, their footsteps soft against the cool stones. Grandpa stopped near the center, setting his walking stick aside. For a moment, he simply stood there, his eyes closed, as if he could see it all happening again.

"This place," Grandpa Joe said, his voice low and steady, "is where Jesus gathered with His disciples for the Last Supper. It was the final meal He shared with them before He went to the cross, and what He did here changed everything—for them, for us, for the whole world."

****

Danny looked around the empty room, his brow furrowed. "It doesn't look like much, Grandpa. Was it special back then?"

Grandpa Joe smiled gently and motioned for them to sit down on a stone bench. "It wasn't special because of the room itself, Danny-boy. It was special because of what Jesus did here. He gave His disciples—and all of us—a gift that we still remember to this day."

Hannah tilted her head. "What kind of gift?"

Grandpa Joe opened his Bible and turned to the Gospel of Luke, his fingers moving across the well-worn pages. "Let me tell you the story. It was during the Feast of Passover, one of the most important celebrations for the Jewish people. They were remembering how God had delivered them from slavery in Egypt—how the blood of the lamb had protected them from death."

Danny sat up straighter. "Like in Exodus, right? When the angel passed over the houses?"

"That's exactly right, Danny," Grandpa said with a nod. "But this Passover was different. Jesus was about to show them—and us—that He was the ultimate Lamb of God. He came to deliver us from a far greater slavery: the slavery of sin."

****

Grandpa began to read from Luke's Gospel, his voice deep and reverent:

"When the hour came, Jesus and His apostles reclined at the table. And He said to them, 'I have eagerly desired to eat this Passover with you before I suffer. For I tell you, I will not eat it again until it finds fulfillment in the Kingdom of God.'"

He paused, looking up at the children. "Can you imagine that? Jesus knew what was coming. He knew that the cross was just hours away, yet He eagerly wanted to share this moment with His disciples. Why? Because He was preparing them for what was about to happen—and for the gift of His sacrifice."

Hannah's voice was soft. "What did He do, Grandpa?"

Grandpa Joe's gaze grew serious, and his voice lowered as he read on:

"He took bread, gave thanks and broke it, and gave it to them, saying, 'This is My body given for you; do this in remembrance of Me.' In the same way, after the supper He took the cup, saying, 'This cup is the new covenant in My blood, which is poured out for you.'"

****

Danny's eyes widened. "Wait… He said the bread was His body? And the cup was His blood?"

"Yes, Danny," Grandpa said, nodding solemnly. "Jesus was using the bread and the cup to show them—and us—what His sacrifice would mean. The bread represented His body, broken for us on the cross. The cup represented His blood, poured out to cleanse us from our sins. He was telling them that He would give everything to save us."

Hannah frowned slightly. "But why would He do that, Grandpa? Why did He have to die?"

Grandpa's voice grew tender, yet strong. "Because, Hannah, sin separates us from God. The Bible says, *'For the wages of sin is death.'* That means we deserved to be punished for our sin. But Jesus, in His love, stepped in and said, 'I'll take their place.' On the cross, He paid the price for our sins so that we could be forgiven. That's why He is called the Lamb of God—He was the perfect sacrifice."

****

The room fell quiet for a moment, the weight of Grandpa's words settling over them like a soft blanket. Danny finally spoke, his voice small but steady. "Is that why we take communion in church? To remember what He did?"

"Yes, Danny-boy," Grandpa said, smiling. "That's exactly why. Communion isn't just a ritual—it's a reminder. Every time we take the bread and the cup, we remember Jesus' sacrifice. We remember His love for us and the price He paid to make us right with God."

Hannah looked down at her hands, thoughtful. "So it's not just about the past—it's about us, too?"

Grandpa nodded, his voice full of warmth. "Yes, Hannah. Jesus' words, *'Do this in remembrance of Me,'* were for His disciples and for all of us who follow Him. Communion reminds us that His sacrifice was personal. He died for *you.* He died for *me.* And when we come to Him with hearts full of gratitude and faith, we are reminded that His love for us is deeper than we can ever imagine."

****

Danny looked around the room again, his voice quiet but certain. "It feels different here now, Grandpa. Like I can almost hear Him saying those words."

Grandpa Joe's face lit up with a gentle smile. "That's because this room isn't just a place, Danny—it's a reminder of the greatest gift ever given. Jesus knew the cross was coming, but He faced it willingly because He loves us. The bread and the cup tell us a story of sacrifice, redemption, and hope."

He paused and placed a hand on Danny's shoulder. "And that hope isn't just for the past—it's for today and forever. Because Jesus didn't just die—He rose again. And one day, He will return, and we will sit at His table in His Kingdom, where there will be no more death, no more sin, and no more tears."

****

The three of them sat in silence for a long moment, the room bathed in soft light. Danny and Hannah could almost see the table, the bread, the cup, and the faces of the disciples as Jesus spoke those words for the first time.

"Grandpa," Hannah said quietly, "I don't think I'll ever think of communion the same way again."

Grandpa Joe's voice was gentle. "That's good, Hannah. Because when we understand what Jesus did for us, we can't help but come to Him with grateful hearts. Communion reminds us of His love, His sacrifice, and His promise—that we are forgiven, and we are His."

****

As they stood to leave the room, Grandpa Joe paused one last time, his voice steady and strong. "Children, never forget this:

Jesus gave everything for us. The bread and the cup are His invitation to remember, to believe, and to trust Him. He is the Savior who laid down His life so that we could live. And because of Him, we have hope—hope that lasts forever."

Danny and Hannah followed Grandpa out of the Upper Room, their hearts full and quiet. The stones beneath their feet seemed to hold the memory of that sacred night, and the words of Jesus echoed softly in their minds:

"This is My body, given for you. Do this in remembrance of Me."

As they stepped into the bright afternoon light, Grandpa Joe whispered a prayer under his breath, one the children couldn't hear but could feel in their hearts:

"Thank You, Lord Jesus, for Your body and blood—for Your sacrifice that saved us all."

CHAPTER 22:
WASHING FEET

The evening sun dipped low as the three of them gathered in a small courtyard just outside their lodging in Jerusalem. The soft sounds of the city lingered in the distance—voices carrying from nearby streets, footsteps echoing on the stone pathways. In the center of the courtyard sat a simple clay basin filled with water and a towel draped across its side.

Danny wrinkled his nose as he noticed the basin. "What's that for, Grandpa?"

Grandpa Joe smiled knowingly, his eyes twinkling with purpose. "You'll see soon enough, Danny-boy. Today, we're going to do something that might seem strange at first, but it's one of the most powerful lessons Jesus ever taught."

Hannah looked at the basin curiously. "Is this like the Last Supper, Grandpa?"

Grandpa Joe nodded, resting his walking stick beside him as he sat on a low bench. "Yes, Hannah. On the night Jesus shared the Last Supper with His disciples, He did something they never expected—something that turned their understanding of leadership, humility, and love upside down."

****

Grandpa Joe motioned for Danny and Hannah to sit beside him on the stone bench. He picked up the Bible from his bag, its pages worn and familiar, and began to read from the Gospel of John.

"Jesus knew that the hour had come for Him to leave this world

and go to the Father. Having loved His own who were in the world, He loved them to the end. He got up from the meal, took off His outer clothing, and wrapped a towel around His waist. After that, He poured water into a basin and began to wash His disciples' feet, drying them with the towel that was wrapped around Him."

Danny's brow furrowed as he listened. "Wait... Jesus washed their feet? That's kind of weird, Grandpa."

Grandpa chuckled softly. "It may seem strange to us, Danny, but back then, people walked everywhere on dusty roads in sandals. Washing feet was a common practice, but it was always done by the lowest servant in the house—not by someone important."

Hannah's eyes widened. "But Jesus wasn't a servant—He was their teacher. He was... well, He was Jesus!"

Grandpa Joe's face grew serious, and his voice dropped lower, full of reverence. "Exactly, Hannah. Jesus was their Lord and their Savior, yet He knelt down to serve them like a humble servant. He was showing them—and us—what true greatness looks like."

****

Grandpa Joe stood up slowly and walked to the basin, picking up the towel. He looked back at the children with a smile. "Now, I know this might make you uncomfortable, but I want to show you what Jesus did that night."

Hannah shifted nervously. "You're not going to wash our feet, are you, Grandpa?"

"Oh, I am," Grandpa said, his voice gentle but firm. "And you'll understand why by the end."

Danny looked unsure but kicked off his shoes and socks anyway. "Well... I guess if Jesus did it, we can try it."

Grandpa knelt by Danny first, his movements slow and deliberate. He dipped his hands into the cool water and gently washed the dust from Danny's feet, drying them carefully with the towel. For a moment, Danny didn't say a word—he just stared down at Grandpa Joe, his face a mix of surprise and humility.

"Grandpa," Danny said finally, his voice quiet, "you don't have to do this."

Grandpa Joe looked up, his face kind. "Neither did Jesus, Danny. But He did it anyway—to teach us what love and service look like."

****

When he finished with Danny, Grandpa moved to Hannah, who offered her feet a bit shyly. Grandpa washed them gently, his voice soft as he spoke. "Do you see, children? Jesus wasn't just washing their feet—He was showing them how to love one another. He was saying, *'If I, your Lord and Teacher, can humble Myself to serve you, then you must serve one another.'*"

He paused, drying Hannah's feet carefully. "This was no small act. Jesus, the King of kings, chose to kneel. He showed us that real greatness isn't found in power or pride—it's found in humility, in serving others, in loving with no thought of ourselves."

****

When Grandpa sat back down, the basin empty, he looked at the children with a steady gaze. "Now listen to what Jesus said to His disciples after He washed their feet:

'I have set you an example that you should do as I have done for you. Very truly I tell you, no servant is greater than his master, nor is a messenger greater than the one who sent him. Now that you know these things, you will be blessed if you do them.'"

Hannah looked at Grandpa, her voice soft but full of thought. "So... Jesus wants us to serve others the way He served us?"

"Yes, Hannah," Grandpa said with a smile. "That's exactly right. Jesus calls us to humble ourselves, to love others, and to put their needs above our own. Whether it's helping a friend, caring for someone who's hurting, or giving our time to those in need, we follow His example when we serve."

Danny leaned back, staring at the basin. "But what if people don't deserve it? What if they're mean or don't care?"

Grandpa Joe's voice grew firm, filled with conviction. "Ah, Danny, that's where the love of Jesus shines brightest. Jesus didn't wait for us to deserve His love—He gave it freely. On that same night, He washed the feet of Judas, the disciple who would betray Him. He served even the one who would turn against Him. That's the kind of love Jesus calls us to have—a love that forgives, that humbles itself, and that gives without expecting anything in return."

****

The three of them sat quietly, the lesson sinking deep into their hearts. The courtyard, once just a quiet place of stone and shadow, now felt holy—set apart by the memory of what Jesus had done and Grandpa's loving reenactment.

"Grandpa," Danny said finally, his voice small but thoughtful, "I think I get it now. Jesus wasn't just telling them to love each other—He was showing them how."

Grandpa smiled, his eyes glistening with joy. "That's exactly right, Danny-boy. The world tells us that greatness comes from power, but Jesus showed us that true greatness comes from serving others. And when we serve, we reflect His love."

****

Hannah looked up, a small smile on her face. "So, it's not about being important—it's about being like Jesus."

Grandpa Joe beamed, his voice warm and steady. "Yes, Hannah. That's it. Jesus said, *'The Son of Man did not come to be served, but to serve, and to give His life as a ransom for many.'* And when we humble ourselves to serve others—no matter how small the task —we follow in His footsteps."

****

As the sun dipped below the horizon, casting a golden glow across the courtyard, Grandpa Joe gathered the basin and towel. Danny and Hannah sat quietly, the weight of the lesson resting on their hearts.

"Grandpa," Danny said, his voice full of wonder, "I want to be more like Jesus. I want to serve like He did."

Grandpa's eyes softened, and he nodded. "That's the best decision you can make, Danny-boy. Follow His example. Love others. Serve with humility. And remember that even the smallest act of kindness can change the world in ways you may never see."

As they stood to leave the courtyard, the simple basin remained, a reminder of a night long ago when Jesus, the King of kings, knelt to wash the feet of His disciples. And in their hearts, Danny and Hannah carried the powerful truth Grandpa had shared—that love is never greater than when it stoops to serve.

And as Grandpa whispered under his breath, almost like a prayer, they felt the truth linger around them:

"Lord, make us humble like You, that we may love and serve as You have loved us."

CHAPTER 23: GETHSEMANE —A NIGHT OF SURRENDER

The Garden of Gethsemane lay quiet under the soft silver light of the moon. Olive trees stood like silent witnesses, their twisted trunks gnarled with age and their branches reaching upward as if in prayer. The ground was uneven and dotted with stones, and the faint scent of earth and leaves lingered in the cool night air.

Grandpa Joe walked slowly, his steps deliberate as he led Danny and Hannah deeper into the garden. His walking stick tapped lightly against the path, breaking the stillness. Neither child spoke. The air here felt heavy—sacred—like it remembered the weight of what had happened in this place so long ago.

"Grandpa," Hannah whispered finally, "why does it feel so... sad here?"

Grandpa Joe stopped near an ancient olive tree, its branches stretching out like arms of sorrow. He turned to face the children, his voice low and full of reverence. "Because, Hannah, this is where Jesus came to pray on the night He was betrayed. It was here, in the Garden of Gethsemane, that He faced one of the hardest moments of His life. It's a place of sorrow... but it's also a place of surrender."

****

They sat together on a low stone wall beneath the shadow of the trees. Grandpa Joe opened his Bible, his hands moving gently over the pages as though they were something precious. "Children, listen carefully, because this moment is one of the most powerful scenes in all of Scripture."

He began to read from the Gospel of Luke:

"Jesus went out as usual to the Mount of Olives, and His disciples followed Him. On reaching the place, He said to them, 'Pray that you will not fall into temptation.' He withdrew about a stone's throw beyond them, knelt down and prayed, 'Father, if You are willing, take this cup from Me; yet not My will, but Yours be done.'"

Grandpa paused, letting the words sink in, his voice thick with emotion. "Right here, under these olive trees, Jesus knelt down and poured out His heart to the Father."

****

Danny shifted uncomfortably. "But why, Grandpa? What was He praying about?"

Grandpa looked up at the moonlit branches above them. "Because Jesus knew what was coming, Danny. He knew the cross was just hours away. He knew He would carry the weight of the world's sin—your sin, my sin, all sin—and it would separate Him from His Father for the first time. That burden was heavier than we could ever imagine."

Hannah's voice was soft. "Didn't He want to go to the cross?"

Grandpa's face grew tender, and he looked into her eyes. "Oh, Hannah, Jesus wanted to do His Father's will—but that doesn't mean it was easy. In His humanity, Jesus felt the weight of the suffering He was about to endure. The Bible tells us that He was overwhelmed with sorrow—so much so that His sweat became like drops of blood falling to the ground. That's how deeply He struggled."

Danny's brow furrowed. "So, He asked God to take it away?"

"Yes," Grandpa Joe said, his voice strong but gentle. "Jesus prayed, *'Father, if You are willing, take this cup from Me.'* The 'cup' was the suffering He would endure—the weight of sin and the punishment He would bear. But then, Danny, Jesus said something that changes everything. He prayed, *'Yet not My will, but Yours be done.'"*

****

Grandpa Joe paused and looked out across the quiet garden. The breeze stirred the leaves above them, whispering through the trees as though echoing Jesus' prayer.

"Do you understand what He was saying, children?" Grandpa asked softly. "Jesus was surrendering completely to the Father's plan. He was saying, 'Lord, this is hard—this is beyond what I can bear—but I trust You. I will do what You ask, no matter the cost.'"

Hannah hugged her knees to her chest, her voice a whisper. "That's so brave, Grandpa."

Grandpa smiled faintly, his eyes glistening in the moonlight. "Yes, Hannah. It was the ultimate act of courage, love, and obedience. Jesus didn't have to go to the cross—He chose to. He surrendered His will because He knew it was the only way to save us. He looked at the suffering ahead and still said, 'Yes.'"

****

Danny looked up at Grandpa, his voice hesitant. "But… wasn't He scared?"

Grandpa Joe turned to face him, his voice low but steady. "Yes, Danny-boy. Jesus was fully God, but He was also fully human. He felt the same emotions we do—fear, sorrow, even anguish. But His love for us was greater than His fear of the cross. That's what makes Gethsemane so powerful: Jesus chose the Father's will over His own, and He did it for us."

He paused, looking at the children. "You see, children, this is where the battle was won. Before He ever reached the cross, Jesus surrendered to the Father's plan right here in this garden. He laid down His will and chose to save us."

****

For a long moment, no one spoke. The garden was quiet, the stillness heavy with meaning. Danny and Hannah looked out at the shadows cast by the trees, as though expecting to see Jesus kneeling there, praying through His tears.

"Grandpa," Hannah said softly, "what does that mean for us? What are we supposed to do?"

Grandpa's voice was full of warmth as he answered. "It means that when we face our own Gethsemanes—when life is hard, when we're afraid, or when we don't understand—we can pray like Jesus did. We can come to God and say, 'Lord, this is hard, but I trust You. Not my will, but Yours be done.'"

He smiled gently at the children. "Jesus showed us how to surrender. He showed us how to trust God, even in the darkest moments. And when we do, we'll find that God gives us the strength to keep going."

****

Danny looked up, his voice small but steady. "Did God answer Jesus' prayer, Grandpa?"

Grandpa Joe's face softened. "He did, Danny, but not in the way we might think. The Father didn't take the cup away, but He sent an angel to strengthen Jesus for what lay ahead. And because Jesus surrendered to the Father's will, we can be saved. That's the beauty of the cross—it wasn't the end of the story. Jesus' victory came through His surrender."

****

The moonlight bathed the garden in silver as Grandpa Joe stood, leaning on his walking stick. "Children, remember this: Gethsemane teaches us that surrender is not weakness—it's the greatest act of trust we can give to God. Jesus showed us that we can bring our fears, our struggles, and our pain to the Father, and He will meet us there with His strength."

Hannah stood, her face thoughtful. "So when we pray, 'Not my will, but Yours,' we're saying we trust God even when it's hard?"

Grandpa Joe nodded, his voice full of love. "Yes, Hannah. And when we trust Him, we'll find peace, just as Jesus did. Because God's plans are always for our good and His glory—even when we can't see it yet."

****

As they began walking back through the garden, Danny looked up at Grandpa. "I think I want to trust God more, Grandpa. Like Jesus did."

Grandpa Joe smiled, his voice full of hope. "That's the best thing you can do, Danny-boy. Trust Him. Surrender to Him. And know that no matter what you face, you'll never face it alone—because Jesus has already walked the path ahead of you."

The wind whispered softly through the olive trees, and the garden seemed to echo with the prayer of the Savior:

"Not My will, but Yours be done."

And as they walked out of Gethsemane, Danny and Hannah carried that prayer with them, understanding for the first time what it truly meant to trust and surrender to God.

CHAPTER 24: THE ARREST OF JESUS

The night had deepened, and the Garden of Gethsemane lay still, its olive trees standing like dark sentinels under the heavy sky. A faint breeze stirred the branches, carrying whispers of what had taken place here only moments before. Danny and Hannah followed Grandpa Joe down a narrow path as he stopped beneath one of the ancient trees.

Grandpa leaned on his walking stick, his face solemn and lined with deep thought. "Children," he began softly, "this very place—this garden that seems so peaceful now—became the setting for one of the darkest moments in history. It was here that Jesus was betrayed, arrested, and taken away like a common criminal. But even in this darkness, God's plan was unfolding."

****

They sat on a stone ledge as Grandpa Joe opened his Bible and turned to the Gospel of Luke. His voice, steady and filled with conviction, broke the silence:

"While He was still speaking, a crowd came up, and the man who was called Judas, one of the Twelve, was leading them. He approached Jesus to kiss Him, but Jesus asked him, 'Judas, are you betraying the Son of Man with a kiss?'"

Grandpa paused, his eyes lifting from the page. "Judas, one of Jesus' closest followers—one of the twelve disciples—had betrayed Him. He led a mob of soldiers, temple guards, and religious leaders into the garden. And how did he betray Jesus? With a kiss—a sign of affection, turned into a symbol of betrayal."

Danny frowned, his voice troubled. "Why would Judas do that, Grandpa? Why would he betray Jesus?"

Grandpa Joe sighed deeply, as though the weight of the question was familiar. "The Bible tells us that Judas had already let greed take root in his heart. He agreed to hand Jesus over for thirty pieces of silver—the price of a slave. But there's something deeper, Danny. Judas misunderstood Jesus' mission. He wanted a Messiah who would overthrow the Romans, not a Savior who would lay down His life. And when Jesus didn't meet his expectations, he turned away."

Hannah's eyes were wide. "But Judas had been with Jesus all that time. How could he do something so terrible?"

Grandpa Joe's voice softened. "It's a hard truth, Hannah. We can walk near to Jesus and still have hearts that are far from Him. Judas saw the miracles. He heard Jesus' teachings. He even broke bread with Him. Yet he chose betrayal. And when he kissed Jesus that night, it revealed where his heart truly was."

****

The breeze whispered through the garden as Grandpa Joe continued. "But Jesus, in His love and mercy, didn't resist. He didn't fight back or call down angels to save Him. He willingly surrendered to the Father's plan."

He turned back to the Bible and read:

"When Jesus' followers saw what was going to happen, they said, 'Lord, should we strike with our swords?' And one of them struck the servant of the high priest, cutting off his right ear. But Jesus answered, 'No more of this!' And He touched the man's ear and healed him."

Danny's mouth dropped open. "Wait—Jesus healed the man who came to arrest Him?"

Grandpa Joe smiled faintly. "Yes, Danny-boy. Even in the middle of betrayal and violence, Jesus showed compassion and mercy. Think about that for a moment. Here was a man who came with the crowd to take Jesus away, yet Jesus healed him. Why? Because Jesus' love never wavered—not even for those who came against Him."

Hannah looked up, her voice quiet. "Didn't anyone stop them? Weren't the disciples afraid?"

Grandpa nodded gently. "They were, Hannah. The disciples didn't understand what was happening. Some wanted to fight, and others were so afraid that they ran away. But Jesus told them, *'Shall I not drink the cup the Father has given Me?'* You see, Jesus knew this was the path He had to take. He had already surrendered His will in prayer, and now He was ready to fulfill His purpose."

****

Danny's voice was almost a whisper. "Why didn't He stop them, Grandpa? He was powerful enough, wasn't He?"

Grandpa Joe's face grew serious, his voice low and steady. "Yes, Danny. Jesus could have stopped them with a single word. He could have called down legions of angels to defend Him. But He didn't—because He came to save us. Jesus wasn't a victim that night. He was a willing Savior. The Bible says, *'The Son of Man came to seek and to save the lost.'* And to save us, He had to be arrested, tried, and crucified. This was the plan from the very beginning."

Hannah looked down, her brow furrowed. "So Jesus let Himself be taken… because He loved us?"

Grandpa's voice was gentle, yet filled with conviction. "Yes, Hannah. He allowed Himself to be betrayed, to be arrested, and eventually to suffer because He knew it was the only way to rescue us from our sin. That night, when the soldiers grabbed Him and led Him away, Jesus was walking the path to the cross— for you, for me, for everyone."

****

The garden seemed to grow quieter as Grandpa Joe's words sank in. The children looked around at the ancient olive trees, imagining the scene—the torches flickering, the clatter of armor, and Jesus standing calm and resolute as the crowd closed in.

"Grandpa," Danny said finally, his voice low, "it doesn't seem fair. Jesus didn't do anything wrong."

Grandpa Joe nodded, his eyes glistening. "You're right, Danny. It wasn't fair. Jesus was innocent—perfect, without sin. But He took our place. The Bible says, *'God made Him who had no sin to be sin for us, so that in Him we might become the righteousness of God.'* Jesus allowed Himself to be betrayed and arrested so that we could be forgiven."

Hannah's voice broke the silence. "What happened to Judas, Grandpa?"

Grandpa's face was solemn. "Judas realized too late the weight of what he had done. The Bible says he was filled with regret, but instead of turning back to Jesus for forgiveness, he gave in to despair. Children, there's a lesson here: No matter how far we've fallen, we must always run back to Jesus. His mercy is greater than our failures."

****

The three of them stood quietly as Grandpa Joe closed his Bible. The garden seemed to hold its breath, as though still mourning what had happened here so long ago.

"Children," Grandpa said softly, "never forget this: Jesus chose this path. He was betrayed, arrested, and taken away—not because He had to be, but because He loves us. He endured the darkness of that night so that we could walk in the light of His grace."

Danny looked up at Grandpa, his voice steady. "So... even when it looked like everything was going wrong, God's plan was still happening?"

Grandpa Joe smiled, placing a hand on Danny's shoulder. "That's exactly right, Danny-boy. Even in the darkest moments, God was working to save the world. And that's the truth we hold on to—when life feels unfair, when we don't understand, we can trust that God is still in control. Jesus was never defeated. He willingly laid down His life so that we could live."

****

As they turned to leave the garden, Danny and Hannah walked more quietly, their hearts heavy with the weight of what they had learned. Grandpa Joe's voice broke the silence one last time, filled with hope and conviction:

"Remember this, children: Jesus wasn't taken that night—He gave Himself willingly. And because of His love, we are never beyond the reach of His grace."

The breeze stirred through the olive trees, and for a moment, the whispers of that night seemed to echo once more:

"Not My will, but Yours be done."

And as they walked away, Danny and Hannah understood a little more of what that surrender had cost—and of the love that made it possible.

CHAPTER 25:
PETER'S DENIAL

The courtyard was nearly empty when Grandpa Joe led Danny and Hannah through its ancient stone archway. A faint chill hung in the air as evening approached, and the flicker of lamplight danced against the weathered walls. The stones beneath their feet were uneven, as though worn down by the footsteps of countless souls over centuries.

Grandpa Joe stopped near an old fire pit, where ashes from long-forgotten fires still seemed to linger. He turned and faced the children, his expression somber yet filled with tenderness. "Children," he began, his voice low and steady, "this is the kind of place where one of the saddest moments in Jesus' story unfolded—a moment that shows us both human weakness and the incredible grace of God."

Danny looked around, his brow furrowed. "What happened here, Grandpa?"

Grandpa Joe leaned on his walking stick and paused, his eyes reflecting the weight of what he was about to say. "This is the kind of courtyard where Peter—the disciple who boldly declared he would never leave Jesus—denied Him. Not once. Not twice. But three times."

****

They sat on a low stone bench near the center of the courtyard. Grandpa opened his Bible and gently flipped through the pages, stopping at the Gospel of Luke. His voice carried the familiar reverence as he began to read:

"Then seizing Jesus, they led Him away and took Him into the house of the high priest. Peter followed at a distance. And when some there had kindled a fire in the middle of the courtyard and had sat down together, Peter sat down with them. A servant girl saw him seated there in the firelight. She looked closely at him and said, 'This man was with Him.' But he denied it. 'Woman, I don't know Him,' he said."

Grandpa Joe paused, his gaze meeting Danny's. "Can you imagine that? Peter—the man who walked on water with Jesus, the man who said he would follow Him to the death—denied even knowing Him."

Hannah frowned, her voice hesitant. "But why, Grandpa? Why would Peter do that?"

Grandpa Joe's voice grew softer, as though speaking to both the children and the silence around them. "Fear, Hannah. Pure, human fear. Peter was afraid. You see, when Jesus was arrested, everything Peter believed was shaken. The man he thought would bring victory was now bound in chains, facing His accusers. And as Peter sat here, warming himself by the fire, he was afraid of what would happen to him if he admitted he knew Jesus."

****

Grandpa Joe continued reading:

"A little later someone else saw him and said, 'You also are one of them.'
'Man, I am not!' Peter replied.

About an hour later another asserted, 'Certainly this fellow was with Him, for he is a Galilean.'
Peter replied, 'Man, I don't know what you're talking about!' Just as he was speaking, the rooster crowed."*

The quiet in the courtyard felt heavier now, as though the stones themselves remembered the sound of that rooster breaking the night. Danny shifted uncomfortably, his voice barely above a whisper. "He did it three times, Grandpa. Just like Jesus said he would."

Grandpa Joe nodded, his voice full of compassion. "Yes, Danny-boy. Earlier that night, Peter had promised Jesus, *'Lord, I am ready to go with You to prison and to death.'* But Jesus knew Peter's heart. He knew Peter's weakness. He told him, *'Before the rooster crows today, you will deny three times that you know Me.'* And that's exactly what happened."

****

The children sat quietly as Grandpa Joe continued, his voice soft and full of sorrow:

"The Lord turned and looked straight at Peter. Then Peter remembered the word the Lord had spoken to him: 'Before the rooster crows today, you will disown Me three times.' And he went outside and wept bitterly."

Hannah looked up, her eyes glistening. "Jesus… looked at him? Right after he denied Him?"

"Yes, Hannah," Grandpa said gently. "Can you imagine that moment? Peter's eyes meeting Jesus', and the reality of what he had done crashing down on him. Peter had failed. He had denied the very One who loved him most."

Danny looked troubled. "I bet Peter thought he was done for. That Jesus would never forgive him."

Grandpa Joe nodded slowly. "It's likely Peter felt that way, Danny. He wept bitterly because he realized the depth of his failure. But here's what I want you to remember: Peter's story didn't end with his denial. It ended with grace."

****

Grandpa Joe's voice grew stronger, filled with hope. "You see, Jesus knew Peter would fail. He knew Peter would stumble under the weight of fear. But He loved Peter anyway. And after the resurrection, Jesus didn't cast Peter aside. He restored him."

Danny leaned forward. "He restored him? What do you mean?"

Grandpa smiled softly, his eyes warm. "In the Gospel of John, after Jesus rose from the dead, He appeared to Peter. Do you know what He did? He asked Peter three times, 'Do you love Me?' And each time Peter answered, 'Yes, Lord, You know I love You.'"

Hannah's voice lit up with understanding. "Three times—just like Peter denied Him three times."

"That's right, Hannah," Grandpa Joe said, his voice full of joy. "For every denial, Jesus offered Peter a chance to reaffirm his love. And then Jesus said to him, *Feed My sheep.*' In that moment, Peter was forgiven and restored. Jesus gave Peter a new purpose —to care for others and share the good news of His love."

****

Danny looked up, his face thoughtful. "So even when we fail, Jesus can still forgive us?"

Grandpa Joe's eyes shone. "Yes, Danny. That's the heart of the gospel. We all stumble, and we all fall short. But Jesus doesn't leave us in our failure. His grace is greater than our mistakes. Just like He did with Peter, He looks at us with love and says, 'Do you love Me? Then follow Me.'"

Hannah hugged her knees to her chest. "It must have been hard for Peter to forgive himself, though."

Grandpa Joe nodded. "That's true, Hannah. Sometimes forgiving ourselves is the hardest part. But Peter learned something important that night—Jesus' love doesn't depend on our perfection. He loves us because of who He is, not because of what we've done."

****

The courtyard grew quiet again as the evening light faded. The children sat with Grandpa Joe, the fire pit before them like a silent reminder of Peter's denial—and Jesus' forgiveness.

"Children," Grandpa said softly, "we are all like Peter sometimes. We make promises to God that we fail to keep. We let fear or pride take over. But Jesus' love never gives up on us. He meets us in our failure and calls us back to Himself."

Danny looked up, his voice steady. "So even when we mess up, Jesus can still use us?"

Grandpa Joe smiled, his face full of hope. "Yes, Danny. Look at Peter. He went from denying Jesus to becoming one of the greatest leaders of the early church. God's grace doesn't just forgive us—it restores us and gives us a new purpose."

****

As they stood to leave, the shadows of the courtyard stretched long across the stones. The sound of the rooster crowing still seemed to linger in the air, but now, so did something greater: the quiet echo of grace.

Grandpa Joe placed his hand on Danny's shoulder as they walked. "Remember, children: God's love is bigger than our failures. When we stumble, we can run back to Him, and He will lift us up again. That's the kind of Savior we have—one who looks at us with love and says, 'Follow Me.'"

And as they stepped through the archway into the fading light, Danny and Hannah carried with them the truth of Peter's story: that failure is never final when grace steps in.

CHAPTER 26: THE VIA DOLOROSA—THE WAY OF SUFFERING

The streets of Jerusalem were alive with the echoes of history. Narrow and winding, the ancient stones beneath their feet seemed to carry the weight of the footsteps that had walked this path for two thousand years. Danny and Hannah followed Grandpa Joe closely as they moved along the *Via Dolorosa*, "The Way of Suffering," where Jesus carried His cross to Calvary. The air felt heavy, not with noise but with a silence that spoke of sorrow and sacrifice.

Grandpa Joe walked slowly, his hand gripping his walking stick tightly. He stopped near a section of the cobbled road, turned back to Danny and Hannah, and motioned for them to sit on a low stone ledge. He removed his hat, as though the very ground here was sacred, and looked up into the quiet sky.

"Children," he said softly, "this is where Jesus walked on the day He gave His life for us. The *Via Dolorosa* is Latin for 'The Way of Suffering,' and it reminds us of what He endured so that we might live. I want you to listen carefully and let the truth of this place sink into your hearts."

****

The three of them sat in silence for a moment, surrounded by the narrow walls of the ancient city. The sunlight barely reached the street below, leaving it cool and shaded. Grandpa Joe opened his Bible, and his voice carried the familiar depth of truth:

"So Pilate handed Him over to be crucified. The soldiers took charge of Jesus. Carrying His own cross, He went out to the place of the Skull (which in Aramaic is called Golgotha)."

He paused, looking at the children with eyes filled with both sorrow and love. "Can you picture it, children? Jesus had already been beaten, mocked, and whipped. The soldiers placed a crown of thorns on His head, and they struck Him again and again. By the time He walked this path, He was weak, bleeding, and in terrible pain. And yet, He carried the cross—our cross—because He knew what it would accomplish."

Danny's face was solemn. "Why did He have to carry the cross, Grandpa? Couldn't someone else have done it?"

Grandpa Joe shook his head gently. "No, Danny-boy. This was Jesus' burden alone. The cross represented the weight of our sin. The Bible tells us that *'He Himself bore our sins in His body on the cross, so that we might die to sin and live for righteousness.'* Jesus carried it because only He could. Only He was sinless. Only He could be the sacrifice to save us."

****

They walked further along the path, stopping again near a small chapel that marked one of the Stations of the Cross. Grandpa Joe turned to face the children. "The Gospel of Luke tells us that as Jesus stumbled under the weight of the cross, the soldiers forced a man named Simon of Cyrene to help Him."

Hannah looked up. "Why did He need help, Grandpa?"

Grandpa's voice softened. "Because Jesus' body was so weak from the beatings and the loss of blood. But even in that moment, there was meaning. Simon carrying the cross reminds us that we, too, are called to carry our crosses. Jesus said, *'Whoever wants to be My disciple must deny themselves and take up their cross daily and follow Me.'"*

Danny looked at Grandpa, confused. "What does that mean? To carry our cross?"

Grandpa Joe's face grew thoughtful, his voice steady. "It means that we choose to follow Jesus, no matter the cost. It means laying down our own desires, our pride, and our plans, and trusting Him fully. It's not always easy, Danny. But Jesus carried His cross for us, and He invites us to follow Him—not in our own strength, but in His."

****

They moved again, stopping near another section of the street. Here, a small stone indentation in the wall was said to mark where Jesus may have leaned as He stumbled. Grandpa Joe touched the wall gently, his eyes distant, as though he could see the Savior there.

"Children," he said, his voice low, "imagine the crowds lining these streets. Some were mocking Him, shouting insults. Others were weeping, unable to understand why this was happening. And through it all, Jesus pressed on. He fell under the weight of the cross, but He got up again—because He knew what was at stake. He knew He was walking this path to save us."

Hannah's voice broke the silence. "Why did He keep going, Grandpa? Why didn't He just stop?"

Grandpa turned to her, his eyes full of warmth and compassion. "Because, Hannah, He saw you. He saw me. He saw all of us. Jesus endured the cross because of His love for us. The Bible says, *'For the joy set before Him, He endured the cross, scorning its shame.'* And do you know what that joy was? It was the thought of you and me being saved. Jesus knew the cross was the only way to rescue us from our sin and give us eternal life."

****

Danny knelt down and ran his hand over the stones of the street. "It feels like... it would've been so heavy, Grandpa."

Grandpa Joe nodded, his voice trembling with emotion. "It was, Danny. And not just the physical weight of the cross, but the weight of the sin of the world. Every lie, every failure, every act of hatred or violence—Jesus carried it all. The perfect Son of God bore the punishment we deserved so that we could go free."

He paused, looking at the children with deep conviction. "That's the depth of His sacrifice. That's the power of His love."

****

They continued walking until they reached a point where the path turned upward, rising toward Golgotha—the place of the Skull, where Jesus was crucified. Grandpa Joe turned to face them, leaning on his stick as his voice rang out with the weight of truth:

"Children, the Via Dolorosa is called 'The Way of Suffering,' but it is also 'The Way of Love.' Every step Jesus took was for us. Every fall, every drop of blood, every insult He endured—He did it because He loves us. The Bible says, *'Greater love has no one than this: to lay down one's life for one's friends.'* And Jesus laid down His life for you and for me."

****

Hannah looked up at Grandpa, her eyes filled with tears. "He must love us so much, Grandpa."

Grandpa Joe's voice softened, his own eyes glistening. "Oh yes, Hannah. More than we could ever imagine. The cross wasn't a place of defeat—it was the place of victory. Jesus' sacrifice on this path brought forgiveness, redemption, and hope to the whole world."

Danny stood up straight, his voice small but sure. "I don't think I'll ever forget this, Grandpa. What He did... it changes everything."

Grandpa Joe smiled, his voice full of hope and joy. "Yes, Danny-boy. It does. And when we remember the Way of Suffering, we must also remember the victory to come. Jesus carried the cross, but He didn't stay in the grave. He rose again. That's why we have hope—because the story didn't end here."

****

As they stood at the top of the path, looking toward the horizon where Golgotha would have been, the wind stirred gently through the streets, carrying the quiet echoes of history.

Grandpa Joe placed a hand on each child's shoulder and whispered, almost like a prayer: "Never forget, children: Jesus walked this road for you. He carried the cross so that you wouldn't have to carry the weight of sin. And because of His sacrifice, we can walk in freedom."

The sun dipped lower in the sky, casting golden light over the ancient stones of the *Via Dolorosa*. Danny and Hannah stood quietly beside Grandpa Joe, their hearts full of awe and gratitude.

And as they turned to leave, they carried with them the truth of this place—that Jesus' steps of suffering were steps of love, leading to the greatest victory the world would ever know.

CHAPTER 27: THE CRUCIFIXION

The air grew still as Grandpa Joe led Danny and Hannah to Golgotha—"the place of the Skull." The ground here was rugged and uneven, the stones sharp and weathered, as though they, too, had been scarred by the events that happened on this hill long ago. The sun hung low, casting a soft golden glow over the site, yet the weight of the place made the children's footsteps slow and reverent.

Grandpa Joe stopped and turned to face them, leaning on his walking stick. His voice, steady and low, broke the silence. "Children, this is Golgotha. This is where Jesus was crucified. This is where the price for our sin was paid, once and for all."

Hannah's small voice broke the stillness. "Grandpa, why is it called 'the place of the Skull'?"

Grandpa Joe looked out over the rocky hill, his face solemn. "Because the shape of the rock here looked like a skull. But, my dear, it is what happened on this hill that has forever marked it in history. This is where the Savior of the world laid down His life for you, for me, and for every soul that would believe."

He paused and opened his Bible, his voice rich and filled with reverence as he began to read from the Gospel of Luke:

"When they came to the place called the Skull, they crucified Him there, along with the criminals—one on His right, the other on His left. Jesus said, 'Father, forgive them, for they do not know what they are doing.'"

****

Grandpa Joe's eyes glistened as he looked up. "Do you hear that, children? Even as Jesus hung on the cross—nails driven through His hands and feet, the weight of His body pulling against the wood—His first words were words of forgiveness. 'Father, forgive them.'"

Danny frowned deeply, his voice a mix of confusion and sorrow. "But, Grandpa, they were hurting Him. How could He forgive them?"

Grandpa Joe took a deep breath and looked at Danny with tenderness. "Because, Danny-boy, Jesus didn't just come to die —He came to save. Even the men who mocked Him and drove those nails into His hands were not beyond His forgiveness. That's the love of God."

Hannah hugged her knees to her chest. "But... why did it have to be so terrible? Why did Jesus have to die like that?"

Grandpa Joe's voice softened, full of compassion. "Because, Hannah, sin is serious. Sin separates us from God. And the Bible tells us that *the wages of sin is death.* But instead of leaving us to face that punishment, Jesus stepped in and took it for us. The cross was the only way to bridge the gap between us and a holy God."

****

The children were quiet as Grandpa continued to read, his voice trembling with the weight of the words:

"One of the criminals who hung there hurled insults at Him: 'Aren't You the Messiah? Save Yourself and us!'
But the other criminal rebuked him. 'Don't you fear God,' he said, 'since you are under the same sentence? We are punished justly, for we are getting what our deeds deserve. But this man has done nothing wrong.' Then he said, 'Jesus, remember me when You come into Your kingdom.'
Jesus answered him, 'Truly I tell you, today you will be with Me in paradise.'"

****

Grandpa looked at Hannah and Danny, his voice steady. "Even in His agony, Jesus showed mercy. A criminal who deserved death looked to Jesus and asked for grace. And do you know what Jesus gave him? Paradise. That's what the cross is about—grace for those who don't deserve it, forgiveness for the guilty, hope for the hopeless."

Danny's voice was hushed. "He forgave him… just like that?"

Grandpa Joe smiled faintly. "Yes, Danny. Jesus doesn't ask us to earn His forgiveness because we never could. He gives it freely to those who believe. The criminal on the cross had nothing to offer—not a lifetime of good deeds, not a clean slate—just a broken heart that turned to Jesus. And that was enough."

****

The wind stirred softly as Grandpa Joe turned to the final verses of Jesus' crucifixion.

"It was now about noon, and darkness came over the whole land until three in the afternoon, for the sun stopped shining. And the curtain of the temple was torn in two. Jesus called out with a loud voice, 'Father, into Your hands I commit My spirit.' When He had said this, He breathed His last."

Hannah's voice broke into the silence. "The sun stopped shining? It got dark?"

Grandpa Joe nodded, his voice trembling. "Yes, Hannah. As Jesus bore the sins of the world, the earth itself seemed to mourn. Darkness covered the land because the Light of the World was dying. But in His final words, Jesus shows us His trust in the Father. He surrendered Himself fully, saying, 'Father, into Your hands I commit My spirit.'"

****

Danny swallowed hard. "So that was it? Jesus died?"

Grandpa Joe's voice was filled with both sorrow and hope. "Yes, Danny. Jesus died. But I want you to hear this: His death was not the end. It was the victory. The Bible tells us that when Jesus died, the curtain in the temple was torn in two. That curtain separated the people from the Most Holy Place, where God's presence dwelled. But because of Jesus' sacrifice, the curtain was torn. The way to God was opened—for everyone."

Hannah looked up, her eyes wide. "So Jesus' death... made a way for us to be with God?"

"Yes, Hannah," Grandpa said softly. "Jesus paid the price for our sin so that we could be forgiven. Through His death, He opened the door to eternal life. The cross isn't a place of defeat —it's a place of redemption. When Jesus said, 'It is finished,' He meant that the work of salvation was complete. The debt had been paid."

****

The three of them stood quietly as the sky turned a soft crimson, the light of evening spreading across Golgotha. Grandpa Joe looked out at the horizon, his voice full of conviction.

"Children, never forget what happened here. Jesus endured the cross because He loves you. He loves you so much that He gave Himself to save you. The Bible says, 'God demonstrates His own love for us in this: While we were still sinners, Christ died for us.'"

Danny and Hannah stood close to Grandpa, their hearts heavy yet full of wonder.

"Grandpa," Danny said softly, "I don't think I'll ever look at the cross the same way again."

Grandpa Joe smiled, his face glowing with hope. "That's good, Danny. The cross changes everything. It's where love won, where sin was defeated, and where grace was poured out for all who believe."

He paused, placing a hand on each of their shoulders. "Remember this: Jesus didn't stay on the cross, and He didn't stay in the grave. The story doesn't end here. The cross leads to an empty tomb—and that's where we'll find our victory."

****

As they turned to leave, the hill behind them was bathed in the soft light of evening. The children looked back one last time, their hearts full of awe and gratitude.

And as Grandpa Joe whispered under his breath, his prayer lingered in the air:

"Thank You, Jesus, for the cross—for Your love that paid the price so we could live."

CHAPTER 28: THE CURTAIN TORN

The soft sounds of the bustling city faded as Grandpa Joe led Danny and Hannah through the ancient ruins of the Temple grounds. The air here was still and heavy, as if time itself lingered to remember what had taken place so long ago. The stones were cracked and worn, but they stood tall, like sentinels guarding a sacred story.

Grandpa Joe paused in front of the site where the Temple once stood, its grand walls long gone but its memory alive. He set his walking stick beside him and turned to face the children. "Children," he began, his voice solemn yet full of excitement, "what happened here is one of the most powerful moments in all of Scripture. It was a moment that changed everything for you, for me, and for all who believe."

Hannah looked up at the empty expanse, her brow furrowed. "What happened here, Grandpa?"

Grandpa Joe rested his hands on his knees and looked at her. "This is where the curtain in the Temple was torn in two. It was God's way of saying that everything had changed because of what Jesus did on the cross."

****

Danny sat on a nearby stone and leaned forward. "Wait... what curtain, Grandpa? What are you talking about?"

Grandpa Joe smiled faintly, his eyes glimmering with understanding. "In the Temple, there was a massive curtain—thick and heavy—that separated the Holy Place from the Most

Holy Place. The Most Holy Place was where God's presence dwelled, and no one could enter it except the high priest, and even he could only go in once a year to offer a sacrifice for the sins of the people."

He paused, letting the weight of those words sink in. "That curtain was a symbol, Danny. It was a reminder that sin separates us from a holy God. You couldn't just walk into God's presence because sin made you unworthy. The people needed a priest, a sacrifice, a way to be made right with God."

****

Hannah's eyes widened. "So... what happened to the curtain?"

Grandpa opened his Bible, turning to the Gospel of Matthew. His voice was rich and steady as he began to read:

"And when Jesus had cried out again in a loud voice, He gave up His spirit. At that moment, the curtain of the Temple was torn in two from top to bottom. The earth shook, the rocks split, and the tombs broke open."

Grandpa Joe looked up, his face glowing with the power of those words. "Children, do you see what happened? At the very moment Jesus died, the curtain in the Temple was torn—not by human hands, but by the hand of God. And it wasn't torn from bottom to top, as though a man had done it—it was torn from *top to bottom*. That was God Himself saying, 'The way is open. My presence is no longer closed off. Come to Me.'"

Danny sat up straighter. "So... people didn't need the curtain anymore?"

Grandpa Joe nodded. "That's exactly right, Danny-boy. The curtain represented the barrier between God and us—a barrier caused by sin. But when Jesus gave His life on the cross, He became the perfect sacrifice. He paid the price for our sin once and for all. The curtain was torn because Jesus removed that barrier forever."

****

Hannah tilted her head, her voice quiet but thoughtful. "Does that mean we can be close to God now?"

Grandpa's face softened, and his voice grew tender. "Yes, Hannah. Because of Jesus, we can come into God's presence freely. We don't need a priest to speak for us. We don't need sacrifices to atone for our sin. Jesus did it all. The Bible tells us in Hebrews, *'We have confidence to enter the Most Holy Place by the blood of Jesus.'* That curtain was torn so that anyone who believes in Him can draw near to God."

Danny frowned slightly. "But… we're still sinners, right? How can we come close to God?"

Grandpa Joe placed a hand on Danny's shoulder, his grip firm and reassuring. "That's the beauty of the cross, Danny. Jesus didn't just forgive our sin—He gave us His righteousness. When God looks at us, He doesn't see our sin anymore. He sees the perfect sacrifice of His Son. Because of Jesus, we are welcomed into God's presence as His children. The Bible says, *'There is now no condemnation for those who are in Christ Jesus.'*"

****

The wind stirred gently, rustling through the ruins as though echoing Grandpa Joe's words. The children sat quietly, taking it all in. Hannah broke the silence first. "So… anyone can come to God now? Not just special people?"

Grandpa's smile widened. "Yes, Hannah. The torn curtain means that salvation is for everyone. Rich or poor, young or old, sinner or saint—it doesn't matter. The way to God is open for all who believe in Jesus. The Bible says, *'For God so loved the world that He gave His one and only Son, that whoever believes in Him shall not perish but have eternal life.'*"

Danny looked down at his hands, then up at Grandpa. "So Jesus dying… it wasn't just about forgiveness. It was about bringing us close to God again?"

Grandpa Joe's eyes glistened with tears, and he nodded slowly.

"That's exactly it, Danny. Jesus didn't just take away our sin—He brought us home. He restored our relationship with God. That's what redemption means: to buy back, to restore what was lost. Because of Jesus, we can call God our Father. We can come to Him in prayer, worship, and trust. The curtain is gone forever."

****

The children sat quietly for a moment, the truth of Grandpa's words sinking deep into their hearts. Danny finally spoke, his voice soft but sure. "So... the torn curtain means we don't have to be afraid to come to God."

Grandpa Joe smiled, his voice full of joy. "Yes, Danny. We don't have to be afraid, and we don't have to stay far away. Jesus opened the door, and He invites us to come. The Bible says, '*Let us then approach God's throne of grace with confidence, so that we may receive mercy and find grace to help us in our time of need.*' That is the promise of the cross—that we can draw near to God."

****

The three of them stood and looked out across the Temple ruins. The air felt different now, as though the weight of history had been lifted by the power of what had happened here.

Grandpa Joe placed his hands on their shoulders, his voice soft yet strong. "Children, remember this: the curtain was torn to show us that nothing—no sin, no shame, no failure—can separate us from the love of God when we believe in Jesus. The way is open. All we need to do is come."

Hannah looked up, her face filled with wonder. "It's like God is saying, 'Welcome home.'"

Grandpa Joe's eyes shone as he nodded. "That's exactly right, Hannah. Through Jesus, God says to every single one of us, 'Welcome home.'"

****

As they walked slowly away from the ruins, the sunlight broke through the clouds, illuminating the ancient stones. Danny looked back one last time and whispered, "Thank You, Jesus, for tearing the curtain."

Grandpa Joe smiled, hearing the quiet prayer. "Amen, Danny-boy. Amen."

And as they left the Temple grounds, the truth of the torn curtain settled deep within their hearts—forever reminding them that because of Jesus, they could come boldly into the presence of a loving God, now and for all eternity.

CHAPTER 29: THE BURIAL OF JESUS

The Garden Tomb was quiet, its peaceful stillness a stark contrast to the sorrow that once hung heavy here. Birds chirped softly from nearby trees, their melodies floating through the calm morning air. Danny and Hannah followed Grandpa Joe into the garden, where flowers lined the pathways and sunlight streamed through gaps in the olive branches.

Grandpa Joe moved slowly, his walking stick tapping lightly against the stone path. He stopped in front of the tomb's entrance—a small, carved opening in the rock, framed by the shadows of history. The children stood beside him, their eyes wide with awe as they gazed at the empty doorway.

Grandpa took off his hat, his voice hushed and filled with reverence. "Children, this is where they laid Jesus after He died on the cross. This tomb—much like the one Joseph of Arimathea offered—was meant to hold the body of the Savior. But it could not hold Him for long."

****

Danny shifted uncomfortably, his voice low. "So... He really died, Grandpa? Jesus really died?"

Grandpa Joe turned to face him, his eyes soft yet steady. "Yes, Danny. Jesus didn't just suffer—He died. The Bible tells us that after the crucifixion, a man named Joseph of Arimathea, a member of the Jewish council who had not agreed with the decision to crucify Jesus, came forward to honor Him."

Grandpa opened his Bible and read gently:

"Now there was a man named Joseph, a member of the Council, a good and upright man, who had not consented to their decision and action. He came from the Judean town of Arimathea, and he himself was waiting for the kingdom of God. Going to Pilate, he asked for Jesus' body."

Grandpa paused, looking at Danny and Hannah. "It took great courage for Joseph to go to Pilate. Most of the religious leaders wanted Jesus gone, and being associated with Him was dangerous. But Joseph loved and respected Jesus. He wanted to honor Him, even in death."

****

Hannah tilted her head, her voice quiet. "But why would Joseph bury Jesus? Wasn't Jesus… alone?"

Grandpa's voice softened. "It must have seemed that way, Hannah. Most of Jesus' disciples had fled in fear. But God had already prepared someone to care for His Son's body. Joseph of Arimathea offered his own tomb—a tomb that had never been used. It was an act of devotion and love."

Grandpa continued reading:

"Then he took the body down, wrapped it in linen cloth, and placed it in a tomb cut in the rock, one in which no one had yet been laid."

Danny frowned, looking at the tomb. "So they just left Him here, Grandpa? That's it?"

Grandpa Joe shook his head gently. "Not quite, Danny. After Joseph placed Jesus' body in the tomb, the Bible says a large stone was rolled across the entrance. Roman soldiers were even stationed to guard it because the religious leaders feared Jesus' followers might try to steal His body."

He pointed toward the carved opening. "Imagine the scene, children. The disciples were hiding, crushed by grief. The women who loved Jesus—Mary Magdalene and others—watched as He was laid here. The sky had grown dark at the cross, and now, silence had fallen. For those who followed Jesus, it must have felt like all hope was gone."

****

Hannah hugged her arms tightly across her chest. "It must have been so sad, Grandpa. They really thought He was gone forever."

Grandpa Joe nodded, his voice low and filled with understanding. "Yes, Hannah. That Saturday must have been the darkest day for them. The Savior they loved—the One they believed would bring God's Kingdom—was dead. They didn't yet understand what was coming. They didn't know the silence wouldn't last forever."

Danny looked into the shadowy tomb entrance, his voice small. "It feels so empty, Grandpa. Wasn't anyone there?"

Grandpa Joe placed a hand on Danny's shoulder. "It may feel empty, but that emptiness carries a message of hope. This tomb didn't hold Jesus for long. But, Danny, I want you to understand the cost of what happened here. Jesus' death wasn't just a tragedy—it was the sacrifice that saved us."

****

Grandpa Joe straightened, his voice growing stronger, full of conviction. "Children, Jesus was buried because He truly died. The Bible says, *'The wages of sin is death.'* That's what we deserved because of our sin. But Jesus took our place. He bore our punishment so we wouldn't have to. And when His body was laid in that tomb, the debt for our sin had been paid in full."

Danny's voice was hushed. "But it still feels so final... like He's just gone."

Grandpa Joe smiled faintly, his eyes full of light. "It must have felt that way to His followers, Danny-boy. But God wasn't finished yet. The Bible says that even when all seemed lost, Jesus' death was part of God's plan from the very beginning. The prophet Isaiah said: *'He was pierced for our transgressions, He was crushed for our iniquities; the punishment that brought us peace was on Him, and by His wounds we are healed.'"*

****

Hannah looked at Grandpa, her voice trembling. "So... this tomb wasn't the end of the story?"

Grandpa Joe's face broke into a tender smile. "No, Hannah. The world thought the story was over. The enemy thought he had won. But this tomb was never meant to hold the Savior. It was only a stopping place. On that dark day, when the stone was rolled in front of the entrance, it seemed like death had triumphed. But, children, remember this: God always has the final word."

Danny looked back at the tomb, his voice soft. "So this... this is where hope was about to begin."

Grandpa nodded, his voice steady and full of joy. "That's exactly right, Danny. This tomb—where grief and silence once reigned—is the same place where the greatest miracle in history was about to happen. Death thought it had won. But three days later, the stone would be rolled away, and Jesus would walk out alive."

****

The three of them stood in quiet awe, the Garden Tomb glowing softly in the light of late afternoon. Grandpa Joe spoke gently, almost as though the words were a prayer.

"Children, never forget the meaning of this place. Jesus died for you. He was buried for you. And because of His sacrifice, sin and death no longer have the final say. The story doesn't end in sorrow—it ends in victory. The tomb is empty now, and because of that, we have hope."

Hannah looked up, her voice full of wonder. "So this is where Jesus' love met our greatest need."

Grandpa Joe smiled, tears glistening in his eyes. "Yes, Hannah. The love of Jesus brought Him to the cross. His sacrifice placed Him in the tomb. And His resurrection will bring Him out of it.

What looked like the end was just the beginning."

****

As they stood in the quiet garden, Danny whispered softly, "Thank You, Jesus, for dying for us."

Grandpa Joe placed his hand on Danny's shoulder. "That's the prayer, Danny-boy. Because of His death, we can live. And because of the empty tomb, we have a hope that nothing can take away."

The wind stirred gently through the trees, and the garden seemed to echo with the promise of what was to come—a promise that would change the world forever.

And as they left the Garden Tomb, the children understood something deeper about the Savior they had been learning about —His love, His sacrifice, and the hope that even death could not silence.

CHAPTER 30: A QUIET REFLECTION

The evening sky glowed with hues of deep orange and soft purple as Danny and Hannah sat on a small bench in the peaceful garden outside the tomb. The weight of the day hung heavy in their hearts, like a truth too great to fully grasp. The hum of Jerusalem's life seemed distant now, muffled by the stillness of the sacred ground.

Grandpa Joe stood a few steps away, leaning against his walking stick. He watched them quietly for a moment, giving the children space to reflect. Finally, he made his way to sit beside them, his voice gentle and steady as he broke the silence.

"Children," he said, "this has been a lot for you to take in, hasn't it?"

Danny nodded slowly, staring down at his hands. "Yeah, Grandpa. It's like… it's so big. I can't stop thinking about everything we've seen."

Hannah looked up, her voice soft but full of thought. "Jesus really went through all of that… for us?"

Grandpa Joe's eyes glistened in the fading light. "Yes, Hannah. Every step He walked, every drop of blood He shed, and every word He spoke was for us. He chose the cross because of His great love for you, for me, and for every person who would believe in Him."

****

The garden seemed to hold its breath as Grandpa Joe looked

out at the tomb. "You know, children, I've been walking with the Lord for many years, but I still marvel at the cost of our salvation. I still get overwhelmed when I remember what Jesus did for me—and for you. We must never take that lightly."

Danny looked up, his voice small. "Grandpa, I don't understand why He would do it. Why would Jesus die for people who don't even love Him back?"

Grandpa Joe turned to face him, his voice full of tenderness. "That, Danny-boy, is the very heart of the gospel. The Bible says, *'God demonstrates His own love for us in this: While we were still sinners, Christ died for us.'* Jesus didn't wait for us to be good enough or deserving enough. He loved us while we were lost in our sin."

He paused, letting the truth settle. "The love of Jesus is not like the love we see in the world. His love is unconditional. It's sacrificial. It doesn't depend on what we do—it depends on who He is. He went to the cross for you because He couldn't bear the thought of eternity without you."

****

Hannah wiped a tear from her cheek, her voice trembling. "But it must have hurt so much, Grandpa. The nails, the crown of thorns... all of it."

Grandpa Joe nodded, his own voice thick with emotion. "Yes, Hannah, it did. The physical pain was beyond anything we could imagine. But there was an even deeper pain—the pain of carrying the weight of our sin. Jesus, the perfect Son of God, bore the punishment that we deserved. He cried out, *'My God, My God, why have You forsaken Me?'* because in that moment, He experienced the separation from the Father that sin causes."

Danny looked up, his eyes wide. "He was separated from God? For us?"

Grandpa Joe nodded solemnly. "Yes, Danny. Jesus took on our sin so that we could take on His righteousness. That's what redemption means—He traded places with us. The Bible says, *'God made Him who had no sin to be sin for us, so that in Him we might become the righteousness of God.'*

****

For a long moment, they sat quietly, the only sound the soft rustle of the olive leaves in the evening breeze. Finally, Grandpa Joe spoke again, his voice full of hope.

"Children, when you look at the cross, you see both the cost of sin and the depth of God's love. Salvation wasn't free—it cost Jesus everything. But He gave it freely because He loves us. He loves *you*. The cross shows us that no matter who we are or what we've done, His grace is enough to cover it all."

Hannah looked up, her face thoughtful. "It's like He gave everything… to give us everything."

Grandpa Joe smiled gently, his heart full of joy. "Yes, Hannah. That's exactly right. Jesus gave His life so that we could have eternal life. And all we have to do is believe—believe that He died for us, that He rose again, and that He alone is our Savior."

****

Danny leaned back against the bench, his voice soft but sure. "It doesn't seem fair, Grandpa. He did everything, and we didn't do anything."

Grandpa Joe nodded. "It may not seem fair, Danny, but that's grace. Grace is when God gives us what we don't deserve. Jesus paid the price we could never pay. And now, because of Him, we can be forgiven, we can be free, and we can know God personally."

Danny looked back at the tomb, his voice a whisper. "So… the tomb means He's not finished yet, right? This isn't the end?"

Grandpa Joe's face lit up with hope. "That's right, Danny-boy. The cross was not the end. The tomb was not the end. Sunday morning is coming. Jesus didn't stay in that tomb—He rose again, and because of that, we have hope that lasts forever. The story of salvation doesn't end in sorrow—it ends in victory."

****

The garden grew darker as the sun dipped below the horizon, the sky now painted with deep purples and blues. Grandpa Joe placed his hands on the children's shoulders, his voice steady and loving.

"Children, what you've seen and heard these past few days is the greatest story ever told. It's not just a story about Jesus' life and death—it's a story about *your* life. Jesus walked this path for you. He carried the cross for you. He faced the tomb for you. And He rose again so that you could have life—abundant, eternal, and full of purpose."

Hannah smiled faintly, her voice full of wonder. "He did all of this… because He loves us."

Grandpa Joe's voice dropped to a whisper, almost like a prayer. "Yes, Hannah. And He still calls to us today, saying, *'Come to Me, all you who are weary and burdened, and I will give you rest.'*"

****

Danny looked up at Grandpa, his voice filled with resolve. "I don't think I'll ever forget this, Grandpa. What Jesus did… it changes everything."

Grandpa Joe beamed, his eyes glistening. "It does, Danny. And now the choice is ours. Jesus gave everything so that we could be saved. All we have to do is believe, trust Him, and follow Him with our whole hearts."

As they stood to leave the garden, the air felt holy—set apart, as though heaven itself had come close. The children walked quietly, their hearts forever marked by the truths they had seen and heard.

Grandpa Joe whispered as they passed the tomb one last time, his voice full of reverence:

"Thank You, Lord, for the cross. Thank You for the empty tomb. Thank You for Your love that saves us still."

And as they walked into the deepening night, Danny and Hannah knew that they would never look at the cross—or their lives—the same way again.

CHAPTER 31: THE EMPTY TOMB

The morning air was cool and crisp as Danny and Hannah walked with Grandpa Joe back to the Garden Tomb. A quiet sense of anticipation hung in the air, like the world itself was waiting to tell its greatest secret. The path they had walked just a day before seemed somehow brighter, the flowers fresher, and the sky clearer, as though creation itself rejoiced.

"Grandpa," Danny said, breaking the silence, "why does today feel so... different?"

Grandpa Joe smiled, his face aglow with a joy that seemed to radiate from deep within. "Because, Danny-boy, this is the day that changed everything. Today we celebrate the greatest victory in history—the day death was defeated, and the grave lost its power."

Hannah's eyes lit up. "It's Easter, isn't it?"

Grandpa Joe nodded, his walking stick tapping softly as they approached the tomb. "Yes, Hannah. Easter morning. The day Jesus rose from the dead. And I want you both to hear what happened here so long ago, the story that brings us hope—hope that lasts forever."

****

They stopped in front of the tomb. Sunlight streamed down, touching the stones and casting a golden glow around the entrance. Grandpa Joe removed his hat, as he had done the day before, and motioned for the children to gather close.

"Do you remember what we talked about yesterday?" he asked. "Jesus' body was laid in this kind of tomb after He died. A stone was rolled across the entrance, and guards were placed to keep watch. It seemed like the end—like hope had been buried with Him."

Danny nodded, staring into the dark entrance of the tomb. "But you said He didn't stay here."

Grandpa Joe's eyes twinkled. "That's right, Danny. He didn't. I want you to listen to how the Bible tells it."

He opened his Bible and began to read from the Gospel of Luke, his voice steady and filled with reverence:

"On the first day of the week, very early in the morning, the women took the spices they had prepared and went to the tomb. They found the stone rolled away from the tomb, but when they entered, they did not find the body of the Lord Jesus. While they were wondering about this, suddenly two men in clothes that gleamed like lightning stood beside them."

Hannah gasped softly, her eyes wide. "Angels?"

Grandpa Joe smiled, looking up. "Yes, Hannah. Angels appeared, bringing the greatest news the world has ever heard."

He continued reading, his voice rising with excitement:

"In their fright, the women bowed down with their faces to the ground, but the men said to them, 'Why do you look for the living among the dead? He is not here; He has risen!'"

****

Danny's mouth fell open. "Wait—what? He wasn't there?"

Grandpa Joe's face shone with joy as he nodded. "That's right, Danny-boy. The tomb was empty because Jesus had risen! The angels told the women, *'He is not here; He is risen!'* Can you imagine the joy and confusion they must have felt?"

Hannah's voice was full of wonder. "But how, Grandpa? How did He come back to life?"

Grandpa Joe leaned forward, his voice soft but firm. "Because Jesus is the Son of God, Hannah. He defeated death by the power of God. Death could not hold Him. The grave could not keep Him. He had told His disciples that He would rise again on the third day, and He kept His word. The resurrection proves that Jesus is exactly who He said He is—our Savior, our Redeemer, and the King who reigns forever."

****

The children stared at the empty tomb, their imaginations alive with the scene Grandpa had described. Danny turned to Grandpa Joe. "So... this is why Easter is so important?"

Grandpa nodded, his voice full of conviction. "Yes, Danny. Easter is the most important day in all of history. Without the resurrection, the cross would only be a sad story. But because Jesus rose from the dead, the cross became a story of victory. It's the proof that sin and death have been conquered forever. The Bible says, *'Where, O death, is your victory? Where, O death, is your sting?'*"

Hannah tilted her head, her voice thoughtful. "So the empty tomb means... we don't have to be afraid of death?"

Grandpa Joe smiled, his eyes shining. "Exactly, Hannah. Jesus said, *'I am the resurrection and the life. The one who believes in Me will live, even though they die.'* Because Jesus rose from the dead, we can have the hope of eternal life. Death is no longer the end for those who believe in Him. It's just the beginning of forever with God."

****

Danny stared back at the tomb, his voice quiet. "It's hard to believe, Grandpa. It's so... amazing."

Grandpa Joe placed a gentle hand on Danny's shoulder. "I know, Danny-boy. The resurrection is the greatest miracle of all. But it's not just a story—it's the truth. Hundreds of people saw Jesus alive after He rose. The disciples who were once afraid became bold preachers of the gospel because they saw Him with their own eyes. They gave their lives to tell the world what they had seen and heard: that Jesus lives."

Danny looked up, his eyes thoughtful. "So if He lives, He's still with us?"

Grandpa Joe nodded, his voice soft but strong. "Yes, Danny. That's the promise of Easter. Jesus is alive, and He is with us. The Bible says, *'Surely I am with you always, to the very end of the age.'* No matter where we are, no matter what we face, we can know that Jesus walks with us because He is alive."

****

The garden grew quiet again, the peaceful stillness wrapping around them like a soft embrace. The children looked at the empty tomb, no longer seeing just a carved-out rock but a symbol of hope, victory, and life.

Grandpa Joe stood, leaning on his walking stick, and turned to face them. "Children, the empty tomb is God's final word on sin, death, and the grave. Jesus is risen, and because He lives, we have hope that cannot be shaken."

Hannah whispered softly, "He is not here… He is risen."

Grandpa smiled, his eyes glistening. "Yes, Hannah. Those are the words that echo through history, words that bring joy to every believer's heart. Jesus is alive, and because of that, everything changes."

****

As they walked slowly back through the garden, the sunlight seemed brighter, the air fresher, and their steps lighter. Danny looked up at Grandpa Joe, his voice clear and confident. "I believe it, Grandpa. I believe Jesus rose from the dead."

Grandpa Joe beamed, his face full of joy. "That's the greatest thing you'll ever believe, Danny-boy. And because of that, you can walk through life with hope, knowing that the One who conquered death walks with you."

Hannah took Grandpa's hand, her face glowing. "He's alive, Grandpa. And we can tell everyone about it."

Grandpa Joe nodded, his voice full of conviction. "That's exactly what we're called to do, Hannah. The empty tomb is not a secret—it's the greatest news the world has ever heard. Jesus is alive, and because He lives, we can face tomorrow."

As they left the garden, the words of the angels seemed to echo on the breeze, filling their hearts with a truth that would never fade:

"He is not here; He is risen!"

And for Danny and Hannah, those words would become more than a story—they would become a reason to live, to believe, and to share the hope of Jesus with the world.

CHAPTER 32: THE ROAD TO EMMAUS

The sun was sinking low as Grandpa Joe, Danny, and Hannah made their way down a quiet, winding path that seemed to stretch endlessly through the countryside. The hills rose gently on either side, dotted with olive trees and wildflowers, their golden hues lit up by the evening light. A peaceful silence surrounded them, broken only by the crunch of their footsteps on the dirt road.

"Grandpa," Danny asked, his voice curious, "why are we walking this long road? What happened here?"

Grandpa Joe smiled and slowed his steps, leaning on his walking stick. "Ah, Danny-boy, this road is a special place. It's called the *Road to Emmaus*. After Jesus rose from the dead, He walked along a road just like this one with two of His followers. But they didn't know it was Him until He revealed Himself to them."

Hannah furrowed her brow. "How could they not recognize Him, Grandpa? Didn't they know what He looked like?"

Grandpa nodded, his voice thoughtful and gentle. "Yes, Hannah. They knew Jesus, but they were so weighed down by grief, so overwhelmed by their own sorrow, that they couldn't see clearly. Sometimes, we are just like those disciples—we get so lost in our troubles that we fail to see Jesus walking right beside us."

****

He paused and opened his Bible, his voice ringing out with a familiar warmth and strength as he began to read from Luke's Gospel:

"Now that same day two of them were going to a village called Emmaus, about seven miles from Jerusalem. They were talking with each other about everything that had happened. As they talked and discussed these things with each other, Jesus Himself came up and walked along with them; but they were kept from recognizing Him."

Danny blinked. "So Jesus was walking right there with them, but they didn't know it?"

Grandpa Joe smiled. "That's right, Danny. Jesus came alongside them, listened to their pain, and walked with them in their sorrow, even though they didn't recognize Him. Isn't that like our Lord? He doesn't leave us alone when we're hurting. He comes alongside us, even when we can't see Him."

****

The three of them kept walking as Grandpa continued, painting the scene with his words. "The disciples on the road to Emmaus were brokenhearted. They had hoped Jesus was the Messiah, but after seeing Him crucified, they thought all their hopes were buried with Him in the tomb. They didn't yet know the full story—*that the tomb was empty, and Jesus had conquered death.*"

Hannah tilted her head thoughtfully. "What did Jesus say to them, Grandpa?"

Grandpa Joe smiled again and turned a few pages in his Bible. "Listen to this." He read:

"He asked them, 'What are you discussing together as you walk along?' They stood still, their faces downcast. One of them, named Cleopas, asked Him, 'Are You the only one visiting Jerusalem who does not know the things that have happened there in these days?'

"'What things?' He asked."

Danny chuckled softly. "Jesus asked them what happened… but He *was* what happened."

Grandpa Joe laughed gently. "Exactly, Danny-boy. Jesus wanted to hear their hearts. Sometimes the Lord does that with us. He wants us to tell Him how we feel, to share our struggles, even though He already knows. That's the kind of Savior He is—He listens to our pain."

****

Grandpa paused, then continued, his voice deep and steady:

"They replied, 'About Jesus of Nazareth. He was a prophet, powerful in word and deed before God and all the people. The chief priests and our rulers handed Him over to be sentenced to death, and they crucified Him; but we had hoped that He was the one who was going to redeem Israel.'"

He stopped reading and looked up at the children, his eyes kind. "Did you hear that, Hannah? *'We had hoped.'* That's what the disciples said. They were so lost in their disappointment that they couldn't see that Jesus was with them. Have you ever felt that way—like God didn't come through the way you expected?"

Hannah nodded slowly. "Sometimes, when things go wrong."

Grandpa Joe nodded back. "We've all been there, Hannah. But Jesus doesn't abandon us in our disappointment. He walks with us. That's what He did on the road to Emmaus. And then, He began to teach them something beautiful."

****

They stopped for a moment as Grandpa Joe looked out over the rolling hills, his voice steady and full of excitement. "The Bible says Jesus explained the Scriptures to them, starting with Moses and the prophets. He showed them how everything pointed to Him—His life, His death, and His resurrection. Can you imagine that? The greatest Bible study ever, taught by Jesus Himself."

Danny's eyes widened. "He showed them that it was all part of God's plan?"

"Yes!" Grandpa said, his voice rising with joy. "God's plan of redemption was woven through the Scriptures all along, and

Jesus revealed it to them step by step. The cross wasn't a mistake —it was the very heart of the plan. The suffering, the sacrifice, the resurrection—it was all God's perfect design to save us."

****

They began walking again, the evening breeze brushing against their faces. Grandpa Joe continued reading:

"As they approached the village to which they were going, Jesus continued on as if He were going farther. But they urged Him strongly, 'Stay with us, for it is nearly evening; the day is almost over.' So He went in to stay with them."

He paused, smiling as he added, "Sometimes we don't realize how much we need the Lord until we invite Him to stay with us. And that's exactly what the disciples did."

****

Hannah leaned closer. "What happened next, Grandpa?"

Grandpa's voice softened, his tone full of reverence. "Listen closely."

"When He was at the table with them, He took bread, gave thanks, broke it and began to give it to them. Then their eyes were opened and they recognized Him, and He disappeared from their sight."

Danny's mouth dropped open. "They finally saw Him!"

"Yes, Danny," Grandpa Joe said, smiling warmly. "The moment Jesus broke the bread, they recognized Him. It was like their hearts caught fire because they knew they had been with the risen Lord."

****

Grandpa Joe closed his Bible and looked at the children, his voice filled with conviction. "Children, here's the truth of the Road to Emmaus: Jesus is with us, even when we don't see Him. He walks with us in our sorrow, He speaks truth to our hearts through His Word, and when we invite Him in, He reveals Himself to us."

Hannah's voice was soft. "It's like He opens our eyes to see Him."

Grandpa nodded. "That's exactly right, Hannah. The disciples said, *'Were not our hearts burning within us while He talked with us on the road?'* When we spend time with Jesus—when we read His Word and invite Him into our lives—our hearts burn with the truth of His love."

****

Danny looked up, his face thoughtful. "So Jesus still walks with us today, Grandpa?"

Grandpa Joe's voice grew soft and steady. "Yes, Danny. Jesus is alive, and He promises to be with us always. Whether we're on the mountaintop or walking through the valleys of life, He is there. The Road to Emmaus teaches us that we're never alone. And when we look back, we'll see that He was with us every step of the way."

****

The sun dipped below the horizon, bathing the hills in soft gold and purple. Grandpa Joe placed his hands on Danny and Hannah's shoulders, his voice low and full of hope. "Remember this, children: when life feels uncertain, when you can't see the way forward, Jesus is walking beside you. Just like He did on the Road to Emmaus, He will reveal Himself to you if you listen, believe, and invite Him in."

As they turned to head back, Danny whispered to himself, "Thank You, Jesus, for walking with us."

Grandpa Joe smiled, hearing the quiet prayer. "Amen, Danny. That's a prayer we can all carry with us."

And as they walked the quiet road together, the truth of Jesus' presence filled their hearts: they were never alone—because the risen Lord still walks beside His people, just as He did on the road to Emmaus.

CHAPTER 33:
THOMAS BELIEVES

The late afternoon sun hung low in the sky as Danny, Hannah, and Grandpa Joe stood in a quiet room in Jerusalem. The stone walls were cool to the touch, and the air was still, heavy with a sense of history and reverence. It was here, Grandpa Joe explained, that Jesus had appeared to His disciples after His resurrection.

Danny ran his hand over the rough stone. "So this is where it happened? Where they saw Jesus alive again?"

Grandpa Joe smiled and nodded. "That's right, Danny-boy. After Jesus rose from the dead, He appeared to His disciples in a room just like this one. But one of them wasn't there that day. His name was Thomas, and he struggled to believe until he saw for himself."

Hannah tilted her head. "You mean *doubting Thomas*? That's what people call him, isn't it?"

Grandpa Joe's expression softened, and he leaned on his walking stick as he began to speak. "Yes, people call him that, but I think Thomas gets a little unfairly judged. Thomas wasn't just a doubter—he was a seeker. He wanted to believe, but he was honest about his struggles. And you know what? Jesus met him right where he was."

****

Grandpa Joe opened his Bible and turned to the Gospel of John. His voice was steady and reverent as he began to read:

"Now Thomas (also known as Didymus), one of the Twelve, was not with the disciples when Jesus came. So the other disciples told him, 'We have seen the Lord!' But he said to them, 'Unless I see the nail marks in His hands and put my finger where the nails were, and put my hand into His side, I will not believe.'"

Danny frowned. "So Thomas didn't believe them? Even after they saw Jesus?"

Grandpa Joe nodded. "That's right, Danny. Thomas struggled to believe because he hadn't seen Jesus for himself. He had watched his Lord crucified—His hands and feet pierced, His side wounded—and it was hard for him to imagine how Jesus could be alive again."

Hannah looked thoughtful. "But Grandpa, isn't that what faith is—believing without seeing?"

Grandpa Joe smiled warmly, his eyes full of pride. "That's exactly right, Hannah. Faith is trusting what we cannot see. The Bible says, *'Now faith is confidence in what we hope for and assurance about what we do not see.'* But God understands our struggles. He knows that sometimes we wrestle with doubt. And instead of scolding Thomas, Jesus came to him."

****

Grandpa Joe continued reading, his voice rising with the beauty of the story:

"A week later His disciples were in the house again, and Thomas was with them. Though the doors were locked, Jesus came and stood among them and said, 'Peace be with you!' Then He said to Thomas, 'Put your finger here; see My hands. Reach out your hand and put it into My side. Stop doubting and believe.'"

Danny's eyes widened. "Jesus showed Thomas the scars?"

Grandpa Joe nodded, his voice tender. "Yes, Danny. Jesus knew Thomas' doubts, and He didn't turn him away. Instead, He invited Thomas to see for himself. He said, 'Put your finger here... stop doubting and believe.'"

He paused, letting the words settle, then continued:

"Thomas said to Him, 'My Lord and my God!'"

****

Hannah gasped softly. "So he believed."

Grandpa Joe's face lit up with a gentle smile. "Yes, Hannah. In that moment, Thomas' faith became real. He didn't just see Jesus —he saw the truth of who Jesus is. He called Him, 'My Lord and my God.'"

Danny looked up, his voice thoughtful. "Jesus didn't get mad at him for doubting?"

Grandpa Joe shook his head. "No, Danny-boy. Jesus didn't scold Thomas—He loved him. Jesus knew what Thomas needed, and He met him with grace. But then Jesus said something very important, something meant for us today."

Grandpa Joe turned back to the Bible and read the words of Jesus:

"Then Jesus told him, 'Because you have seen Me, you have believed; blessed are those who have not seen and yet have believed.'"

****

Hannah whispered, "That's us, isn't it, Grandpa? We haven't seen Jesus, but we still believe."

Grandpa Joe's eyes shone with joy. "Yes, Hannah. That's you, and that's me. We are the ones Jesus was talking about—the ones who believe without seeing. And He calls us blessed because of our faith."

He paused, looking at the children. "You see, children, faith isn't about having all the answers or never wrestling with doubt. Faith is trusting in Jesus, even when we can't see Him. It's believing in His promises, even when life is hard. It's knowing that He is with us, just as He promised, *'I will never leave you nor forsake you.'"*

****

Danny looked down, his voice quiet but honest. "Sometimes I feel like Thomas, Grandpa. Sometimes I wonder if it's all true."

Grandpa Joe placed a hand on Danny's shoulder, his voice kind and steady. "Danny, you're not alone. Many people struggle with doubts at some point. But don't be afraid of your questions. Bring them to Jesus, just like Thomas did. He will meet you where you are, and He will show you His truth."

He smiled gently. "And when you're struggling to see Him, remember this: the scars in His hands, the wounds in His side—they are proof of His love for you. Jesus died for you, and He rose again so you could have life. That's the truth you can always hold onto."

****

Hannah looked up, her face thoughtful. "I think it's amazing that Jesus didn't give up on Thomas."

Grandpa Joe nodded. "That's the kind of Savior we serve, Hannah. He doesn't give up on us. He meets us in our doubts, and He turns our doubts into faith. Just like He did with Thomas, Jesus is always reaching out to us, saying, 'Stop doubting and believe.'"

Danny smiled faintly. "So we can trust Him even when we can't see Him?"

Grandpa Joe beamed. "Yes, Danny. That's what faith is all about. Trusting that Jesus is who He says He is. Trusting that He's alive, that He loves you, and that He's with you every step of the way."

****

As they stepped back into the sunlight, Grandpa Joe turned to face the children. "Children, don't ever forget the story of Thomas. It's a story of grace and a story of hope. Jesus loves us, even when we doubt. And when we choose to believe, even without seeing, He calls us blessed."

Danny and Hannah walked quietly for a moment, the truth

settling in their hearts. Finally, Danny looked up at Grandpa and said with quiet resolve, "I believe, Grandpa. I believe Jesus is alive."

Grandpa Joe's face shone with joy. "That's the greatest decision you'll ever make, Danny-boy. And no matter what comes, you can hold onto that truth: Jesus lives, and He is with you."

As they continued down the path, the words of Jesus seemed to echo in their hearts:

"Blessed are those who have not seen and yet have believed."

And for Danny and Hannah, faith no longer felt like a distant idea. It was real. It was personal. And it was alive—just like their Savior.

CHAPTER 34: JESUS APPEARS BY THE SEA

The morning sun shimmered across the surface of the Sea of Galilee as soft waves lapped gently against the shore. Grandpa Joe, Danny, and Hannah stood at the water's edge, their shoes sinking slightly into the damp sand. The air smelled fresh, with a faint saltiness carried on the breeze. Fishing boats bobbed in the distance, and the whole scene seemed timeless, untouched by the centuries that had passed.

"This is the Sea of Galilee," Grandpa Joe said, his voice low and reverent. "The very waters where Jesus walked, taught, and calmed the storm. But today, I want to tell you about another moment on this sea—one that speaks of grace, forgiveness, and a love that never gives up."

Danny skipped a small stone across the water. "What happened here, Grandpa?"

Grandpa Joe smiled as he looked out over the waves. "It's the story of Peter—one of Jesus' closest disciples. Peter was bold, loyal, and strong. But Peter also made a mistake—a mistake he thought could never be forgiven. And yet, Jesus met him right here, on the shores of this very sea, to restore him."

****

Hannah glanced up at Grandpa Joe. "Is this about when Peter denied Jesus?"

Grandpa nodded solemnly. "Yes, Hannah. The night Jesus was arrested, Peter followed Him to the courtyard where He was being tried. Peter had promised, *'Even if I have to die with You, I will never disown You.'* But fear gripped Peter's heart. Three times, people accused him of being one of Jesus' followers, and three times Peter denied it."

Danny frowned. "He said he didn't even know Jesus?"

"Yes, Danny," Grandpa Joe replied. "And the third time, the Bible tells us Peter swore, *'I don't know the man!'* Just then, a rooster crowed, just as Jesus had told Peter it would. And Peter remembered. The Bible says he went outside and wept bitterly."

Hannah's eyes softened. "He must have felt awful."

Grandpa Joe turned to face them, his expression kind but serious. "He did, Hannah. Can you imagine the weight of that guilt? Peter had loved Jesus, walked with Him, and promised to stand by Him no matter what. But when the moment came, Peter failed. And he thought that failure was the end of his story."

****

Grandpa looked back out at the sea, as if seeing Peter's story unfold before him. "But here's where the grace of God changes everything. After Jesus rose from the dead, He appeared to His disciples several times. One of those moments happened right here, by the Sea of Galilee."

He opened his Bible and began to read from John 21, his voice deep and steady:

"Early in the morning, Jesus stood on the shore, but the disciples did not realize that it was Jesus. He called out to them, 'Friends, haven't you any fish?'

"'No,' they answered.

"He said, 'Throw your net on the right side of the boat and you will find some.' When they did, they were unable to haul the net in because of the large number of fish."

Danny's eyes lit up. "Wait! That's like when Jesus first called Peter to follow Him, isn't it?"

Grandpa Joe smiled. "You're exactly right, Danny-boy. Years earlier, Jesus told Peter to cast his net, and Peter hauled in a miraculous catch of fish. That was when Peter first knew who Jesus really was. And now, after everything Peter had done —after his denial—Jesus performed the same miracle. He was reminding Peter of who He is, and of the calling He had placed on Peter's life."

****

Hannah leaned in closer. "What happened next, Grandpa?"

Grandpa Joe continued reading:

"Then the disciple whom Jesus loved said to Peter, 'It is the Lord!' As soon as Simon Peter heard him say, 'It is the Lord,' he wrapped his outer garment around him and jumped into the water."

Danny grinned. "Peter jumped out of the boat?"

Grandpa Joe chuckled softly. "He sure did, Danny. That's Peter for you—passionate and impulsive. He couldn't wait another moment. He had to get to Jesus. And when the other disciples followed in the boat, they found Jesus waiting for them on the shore, cooking breakfast over a fire."

****

Hannah tilted her head. "Jesus made them breakfast?"

"Yes, Hannah," Grandpa Joe said with a smile. "Isn't that just like Him? After everything that had happened, Jesus didn't scold them or lecture them. He fed them. He welcomed them. And then He turned to Peter."

He closed the Bible for a moment and spoke softly. "Imagine Peter sitting there, the fire crackling, the smell of fish in the air. Peter must have been so nervous—so ashamed of what he had done. But Jesus looked at Peter and said, *'Simon, son of John, do you love Me?'*"

Hannah whispered, "What did Peter say?"

Grandpa Joe smiled. "Peter said, *'Yes, Lord, You know that I love You.'* But Jesus didn't stop there. He asked Peter the same question three times: *'Do you love Me?'* And each time, Peter answered, 'Yes, Lord, You know I love You.'"

****

Danny frowned, thinking it through. "Why did Jesus ask him three times?"

Grandpa Joe's voice was gentle and steady. "Because Peter had denied Jesus three times. And now, Jesus was giving Peter the chance to reaffirm his love three times. With each question, Jesus wasn't condemning Peter—He was restoring him. He was lifting Peter out of his guilt and reminding him of his purpose."

He paused, then added, "After Peter answered, Jesus said, *'Feed My sheep.'* That was Jesus' way of saying, 'Peter, I'm not done with you. I still have a plan for you. You're forgiven, and I'm calling you to care for My people.'"

****

Hannah's voice was soft. "So Jesus gave Peter a second chance?"

Grandpa Joe nodded, his eyes shining. "That's exactly right, Hannah. Jesus gave Peter a fresh start. He showed Peter—and all of us—that no mistake is too big for God's grace. The cross paid for our sin, and the resurrection gives us new life. No matter what we've done, Jesus is ready to forgive and restore us, just as He did for Peter."

****

The three of them stood quietly for a moment, the gentle waves of the Sea of Galilee lapping at their feet. Finally, Danny looked up at Grandpa Joe. "So even when we mess up, Jesus still loves us?"

Grandpa Joe smiled warmly, placing a hand on Danny's shoulder. "Yes, Danny-boy. That's the beauty of God's grace. We all fail, but Jesus doesn't give up on us. He meets us right where we are, and He says, 'Do you love Me? Follow Me.' And when we say yes, He restores us and gives us a purpose."

****

Hannah stared out at the water, her voice thoughtful. "Peter must have felt so relieved to know Jesus still loved him."

Grandpa Joe nodded. "He did, Hannah. And do you know what? Peter went on to become one of the greatest leaders of the early church. He preached boldly about Jesus, and he never forgot the grace he had been shown."

****

As the sun dipped lower in the sky, Grandpa Joe turned back to Danny and Hannah. "Children, the story of Peter shows us that no matter how far we fall, Jesus is always ready to lift us up. He calls us to Himself, forgives us, and gives us a new beginning."

Danny's face broke into a smile. "That's pretty amazing, Grandpa."

Grandpa Joe nodded, his voice full of conviction. "Yes, Danny. The grace of Jesus is amazing. And it's a grace that is offered to you, to me, and to anyone who will come to Him."

****

As they turned to walk along the shore, the soft sound of the waves seemed to echo Jesus' words:

"Do you love Me? Follow Me."

And for Danny and Hannah, those words became a call not just for Peter, but for themselves—a call to follow the One who forgives, restores, and loves without end.

CHAPTER 35: THE GREAT COMMISSION

The soft breeze carried the sounds of rustling leaves as Grandpa Joe, Danny, and Hannah climbed a small hill overlooking the Sea of Galilee. Below them, the waters stretched out like a shimmering sheet of glass, and in the distance, the faint outline of villages could be seen. Birds soared above them, and the sunlight seemed to glow with a warmth that matched the joy in Grandpa Joe's face.

"Children," Grandpa Joe began, as he leaned on his walking stick and gazed out at the vast horizon, "this is where it all began —and where Jesus gave His followers a mission that still stands to this day."

Danny looked out over the water, shielding his eyes from the sun. "What mission, Grandpa?"

Grandpa Joe turned to face them, his expression serious yet filled with joy. "It's called the **Great Commission**—Jesus' final instructions before He ascended into heaven. After the resurrection, Jesus gathered His disciples on a mountain not far from here and gave them a command that would change the world forever."

****

Hannah tilted her head, curiosity lighting her face. "What did He tell them to do?"

Grandpa Joe opened his well-worn Bible and gently turned to the Gospel of Matthew. His voice took on a deep, steady rhythm as he read:

"Then Jesus came to them and said, 'All authority in heaven and on earth has been given to Me. Therefore go and make disciples of all nations, baptizing them in the name of the Father and of the Son and of the Holy Spirit, and teaching them to obey everything I have commanded you. And surely I am with you always, to the very end of the age.'"

****

Danny frowned slightly. "So… Jesus wanted them to go everywhere and tell people about Him?"

"Yes, Danny-boy," Grandpa Joe said, nodding. "Jesus had spent three years teaching His disciples, showing them the truth of God's love, and now He was sending them out. He was saying, 'Take what I've taught you and share it—not just with a few people, but with the whole world.'"

Hannah's voice grew thoughtful. "Why did Jesus say 'all nations,' Grandpa? Didn't He just teach people here in Israel?"

Grandpa Joe smiled, his eyes shining with a quiet excitement. "That's a wonderful question, Hannah. When Jesus came, He brought good news not just for one group of people, but for *everyone*—every nation, every tribe, every language. You see, the gospel is for the whole world because God loves the whole world. That's why Jesus said, *'Go and make disciples of all nations.'"*

****

Grandpa Joe paused, looking at both children. "Think about it this way: Jesus had risen from the dead, proving that He was the Son of God. But there were so many people who didn't know Him yet—people who had never heard about His love, His sacrifice, and His victory over sin and death. So Jesus sent His followers to tell them."

Danny kicked a small stone near his foot. "But how could just a few people tell the whole world, Grandpa? That sounds impossible."

Grandpa Joe nodded, his voice steady and reassuring. "It may have seemed impossible, Danny, but with God, all things are possible. Jesus promised His disciples something very important —He promised them that He would be with them, *always.* They wouldn't be doing this work alone. The Holy Spirit would give them power and boldness to share the good news."

****

Hannah smiled faintly. "So Jesus was asking them to keep telling His story?"

Grandpa Joe's face beamed with joy. "Exactly, Hannah. The story of salvation—the story of how Jesus died for our sins, rose from the dead, and offers us eternal life—is too good to keep to ourselves. Jesus was calling His followers to be messengers, to go out and teach others about Him, to baptize them, and to help them live as His disciples."

Danny's brow furrowed in thought. "Grandpa, what does it mean to make disciples?"

Grandpa Joe leaned in closer, his voice gentle but full of conviction. "To make disciples means to help people know Jesus and follow Him. It's not just about sharing the gospel once and walking away—it's about walking alongside others, teaching them about God's Word, and helping them grow in their faith."

He smiled as he added, "You see, Danny, a disciple isn't just someone who believes in Jesus. A disciple is someone who learns from Him, loves Him, and lives like Him. And when we make disciples, we're helping others find the joy of knowing Jesus too."

****

Hannah sat quietly for a moment, looking out over the water. "So Jesus gave them this big mission. Did they do it?"

Grandpa Joe nodded, his voice steady and strong. "Oh, yes, Hannah. The disciples took Jesus' words to heart. They traveled far and wide, preaching the gospel, teaching people about Jesus, and baptizing them. And because they obeyed the Great Commission, the good news spread—across countries, across continents, and across centuries. That's why we know about Jesus today. Someone, somewhere, shared the gospel with us."

Danny's eyes widened. "And now it's our turn, isn't it?"

Grandpa Joe's face lit up with joy. "Yes, Danny-boy! That's the beauty of the Great Commission—it's not just for the disciples back then. It's for all of us today. Jesus calls each of us to share His love with the people around us. Whether it's our family, our friends, or even people in other parts of the world, we are all part of His mission."

****

Hannah's voice was quiet but full of wonder. "It sounds like a big responsibility, Grandpa."

Grandpa Joe nodded solemnly. "It is, Hannah. But we don't do it alone. Remember what Jesus said: *'Surely I am with you always, to the very end of the age.'* When we step out in faith to share the gospel, Jesus is right there with us. He gives us courage when we're afraid and strength when we're weak. He walks beside us every step of the way."

****

The three of them stood together in the quiet, looking out over the vast horizon. Grandpa Joe spoke again, his voice deep and full of hope. "Children, the Great Commission is the most important mission in the world. Jesus came to save us, and now He asks us to tell others about that salvation. It's not just a suggestion—it's a command. But it's also a privilege. We get to be part of God's work to bring hope, forgiveness, and eternal life to those who need Him."

Danny turned to Grandpa, his voice firm. "I want to do that, Grandpa. I want to tell people about Jesus."

Hannah smiled and nodded. "Me too. I want everyone to know how much He loves them."

Grandpa Joe's face beamed as he looked at them both. "That's what it's all about, children. The world needs to hear about Jesus, and He's counting on us to share His story. So wherever you go, whatever you do, remember these words: *'Go and make disciples of all nations.'*"

****

As they started back down the hill, the breeze carried the faint sound of waves lapping at the shore. Danny glanced back over his shoulder and whispered to himself, "Jesus is with us… always."

Grandpa Joe smiled, hearing the quiet words. "Yes, Danny. And because He is, we can go forward with boldness and joy, sharing the greatest news the world has ever heard."

The three of them walked on, the mission of the Great Commission ringing in their hearts—a mission of love, hope, and a promise that Jesus would never leave them.

CHAPTER 36: ASCENSION ON THE MOUNT OF OLIVES

The golden afternoon sun bathed the Mount of Olives in light as Grandpa Joe, Danny, and Hannah climbed the ancient hillside. Olive trees dotted the landscape, their twisted trunks standing as silent witnesses to centuries of history. The air carried a faint breeze, gentle and refreshing, as if to honor the sacred events that once took place here.

"This is it, children," Grandpa Joe said, pausing to catch his breath and take in the view. "The Mount of Olives. A place of great significance throughout the Bible. And it was from right here that Jesus left this earth—ascending into heaven with a promise that has carried hope through the ages."

Hannah looked around at the peaceful surroundings, her voice soft with wonder. "Jesus really ascended… from here?"

Grandpa Joe nodded, his eyes shining with reverence. "Yes, Hannah. This very place where we stand was the setting for Jesus' final moments with His disciples before He returned to His Father. It was a moment that changed everything—not as an ending, but as a beginning. Let me tell you the story."

****

They found a small, shaded spot near a cluster of olive trees where they could sit. Grandpa Joe leaned on his walking stick and opened his Bible to the book of Acts, his voice rich with purpose.

"Then they gathered around Him and asked Him, 'Lord, are You at this time going to restore the kingdom to Israel?' He said to them: 'It is not for you to know the times or dates the Father has set by His own authority. But you will receive power when the Holy Spirit comes on you; and you will be My witnesses in Jerusalem, and in all Judea and Samaria, and to the ends of the earth.'"

Danny tilted his head. "So Jesus told them their job wasn't done yet?"

Grandpa Joe smiled. "That's right, Danny-boy. The disciples still didn't fully understand what Jesus was doing. They thought He might restore Israel as a political kingdom right then and there. But Jesus told them something much greater: they were to carry His message to the ends of the earth. And He promised they wouldn't do it alone—He would send the Holy Spirit to empower them."

****

Hannah leaned forward. "Then what happened, Grandpa?"

Grandpa Joe's voice grew even softer, almost as if he could see the scene unfolding before him. "Listen to this," he said, reading from Acts 1:9:

"After He said this, He was taken up before their very eyes, and a cloud hid Him from their sight."

Danny's eyes widened. "Wait—Jesus just… went up? Into the sky?"

"Yes, Danny," Grandpa Joe replied, his voice steady and full of awe. "The Bible says that as His disciples watched, Jesus began to rise—lifted up into heaven until a cloud hid Him from view. Can you imagine what that must have been like? To see the One who had walked beside you—your Savior, your Lord—ascending into glory before your very eyes?"

Hannah whispered, "I think I'd just stand there, staring."

Grandpa Joe smiled. "You wouldn't have been the only one, Hannah. The disciples were so amazed that they just stood there, looking up at the sky. But God had a message for them even then."

****

He continued reading:

"They were looking intently up into the sky as He was going, when suddenly two men dressed in white stood beside them. 'Men of Galilee,' they said, 'why do you stand here looking into the sky? This same Jesus, who has been taken from you into heaven, will come back in the same way you have seen Him go into heaven.'"

Hannah's eyes widened. "They were angels, weren't they?"

Grandpa Joe nodded. "Yes, Hannah. Angels brought a message of hope to the disciples: Jesus would return. The same way He ascended into heaven, He will come back one day—this time as King of Kings and Lord of Lords."

****

Danny looked up at the sky, as if trying to picture it. "So Jesus promised He'd come back?"

Grandpa Joe's voice filled with conviction. "That's right, Danny. And that's a promise we still hold onto today. Jesus is coming again. The Bible tells us that He will return to judge the living and the dead, to bring justice to the world, and to make all things new. For those who believe in Him, that day will be a day of joy and triumph."

Hannah's voice was thoughtful. "So we're still waiting for Him?"

"Yes, Hannah," Grandpa Joe replied. "But waiting doesn't mean sitting still. Remember what Jesus said? 'You will be My witnesses.' While we wait for His return, we have a mission: to share the gospel, to love others, and to live as His disciples. The disciples didn't stand staring at the sky forever—they went out into the world, just as Jesus told them."

****

Grandpa Joe paused, looking out over the horizon as the afternoon light glowed golden against the hills. "Children, the ascension wasn't the end of Jesus' work—it was the beginning of the church. Jesus left, but He sent the Holy Spirit to live within every believer, to guide us, empower us, and help us carry out His mission."

Danny looked up at Grandpa, his voice filled with curiosity. "Do you think Jesus will come back soon?"

Grandpa Joe smiled gently. "The Bible says no one knows the day or the hour—only the Father knows. But the Bible also tells us to be ready, to live each day as if Jesus might return tomorrow. And while we wait, we're called to live with hope, with faith, and with purpose."

****

Hannah sat quietly, staring out at the Sea of Galilee. "It's kind of amazing to think He's coming back. It makes me want to be ready."

Grandpa Joe's face lit up with a warm smile. "That's exactly how Jesus wants us to live, Hannah. The Bible tells us, *'So you also must be ready, because the Son of Man will come at an hour when you do not expect Him.'* Being ready means trusting Him, following Him, and sharing His love with others. It means living for His glory every single day."

****

The three of them stood, looking out over the Mount of Olives in the fading light. The breeze seemed to carry whispers of the promise that had been given so long ago. Grandpa Joe turned to the children and spoke softly, his voice full of hope:

"Children, the Mount of Olives reminds us that Jesus is alive, reigning in heaven, and one day He will return. That's not just a story—it's the truth. And until that day comes, we have a job to do: to share His message with a world that needs Him. He is coming again, and when He does, every knee will bow and every tongue will confess that Jesus Christ is Lord."

Danny and Hannah nodded quietly, their hearts full of wonder and anticipation.

****

As they walked back down the hill, Grandpa Joe's words echoed in their minds:

"This same Jesus... will come back."

And for Danny and Hannah, the Mount of Olives became more than just a beautiful place. It became a reminder of a promise that had been made—and a promise that would one day be fulfilled.

CHAPTER 37: A PROMISE FULFILLED

The sun dipped low in the sky as Grandpa Joe, Danny, and Hannah sat on a stone bench near the Mount of Olives. The golden light bathed the hills and valleys in a warm glow, and the quiet seemed to stretch forever, as if the earth itself was reflecting on all it had seen. Grandpa Joe leaned on his walking stick, his Bible open on his lap, and gazed thoughtfully into the horizon.

"Children," he began softly, "everything we've seen, everything we've talked about, points to one thing: God's perfect plan. From the first prophecy to the empty tomb, every promise about Jesus has been fulfilled."

Danny tilted his head. "What do you mean, Grandpa? What promises?"

Grandpa Joe smiled gently, his voice steady as he answered. "The Bible is full of promises—prophecies written hundreds, even thousands of years before Jesus was born. Promises that told us exactly who He would be, what He would do, and how He would save the world."

****

Hannah's eyes widened. "So the things Jesus did... they were all part of God's plan?"

"Yes, Hannah," Grandpa Joe replied, his voice rich with conviction. "Every single event was foretold. Let me show you." He opened his Bible, flipping through its pages, and stopped at the book of Isaiah. "This was written more than 700 years before

Jesus came."

He began to read, his voice steady and reverent:

"But He was pierced for our transgressions, He was crushed for our iniquities; the punishment that brought us peace was on Him, and by His wounds we are healed."

Danny frowned slightly, trying to process the words. "That sounds like what happened to Jesus on the cross."

Grandpa Joe nodded. "Exactly, Danny-boy. Long before Jesus was born, God spoke through the prophet Isaiah to describe how the Messiah would suffer and die for our sins. Jesus fulfilled that prophecy completely when He gave His life on the cross."

****

Hannah leaned forward, her voice full of curiosity. "Were there other prophecies too?"

Grandpa Joe smiled, flipping through the pages of his Bible. "Oh, yes, Hannah. Many, many others. Let me show you a few of them."

He turned to Micah and read:

"But you, Bethlehem Ephrathah, though you are small among the clans of Judah, out of you will come for Me one who will be ruler over Israel, whose origins are from of old, from ancient times."

Danny's eyes widened. "Bethlehem! That's where Jesus was born."

"Exactly," Grandpa Joe said with a nod. "Micah prophesied that the Messiah would be born in Bethlehem—and that's exactly where Jesus was born, just as God had promised."

He turned to the Psalms and read another passage:

"They divide My clothes among them and cast lots for My garment."

Hannah whispered, "That's what happened at the cross, isn't it?"

"Yes, Hannah," Grandpa Joe replied, his voice soft but filled with awe. "When Jesus was crucified, the Roman soldiers cast lots for His clothing. David wrote those words a thousand years earlier, and yet every detail came true."

****

Grandpa Joe closed the Bible for a moment and looked at the children. "Children, do you see what this means? These prophecies weren't accidents. They weren't guesses. They were part of God's perfect plan to send His Son to save us. From His birth in Bethlehem to His death on the cross to His resurrection from the tomb, every detail happened exactly as God said it would."

Danny stared at Grandpa, his voice quiet but firm. "So Jesus really was the Messiah?"

"Yes, Danny-boy," Grandpa Joe said, his eyes shining with joy. "Jesus is the Messiah. He is the Savior God promised, the One who fulfilled every prophecy written about Him. And do you know what that shows us?"

"What?" Hannah asked softly.

Grandpa Joe's voice grew stronger. "It shows us that God keeps His promises. Every single one. The Bible says, *'For no matter how many promises God has made, they are 'Yes' in Christ.'* Jesus is the proof that God's Word is true, that His plan is perfect, and that we can trust Him completely."

****

The three of them sat quietly for a moment, the truth of Grandpa Joe's words settling deep into their hearts. Finally, Danny broke the silence. "So, if God kept all those promises, does that mean we can trust Him to keep His promises to us too?"

Grandpa Joe smiled, his face full of warmth and assurance. "Yes, Danny. That's exactly what it means. God's faithfulness in the past is our confidence for the future. He has promised to be with us, to forgive us, and to give us eternal life through Jesus. And He has promised that one day, Jesus will return—just as He said He would."

Hannah's voice was full of wonder. "It's amazing how everything fits together, Grandpa. It's like a big puzzle, and Jesus is the piece that makes it all complete."

Grandpa Joe beamed. "That's a perfect way to put it, Hannah. Jesus is the fulfillment of God's promises. He is the Lamb of God who takes away the sin of the world. He is the Good Shepherd who lays down His life for His sheep. And He is the Risen King who reigns forever."

****

Danny looked up at the sky, his voice thoughtful. "So the story of Jesus didn't just start when He was born. It started way before that."

Grandpa Joe nodded, his voice soft but strong. "Yes, Danny. The story of Jesus began long before Bethlehem. It began in the heart of God, who loved us so much that He set a plan in motion to save us. The Bible tells us that Jesus was 'the Lamb slain from the foundation of the world.' That means God's plan to send Jesus was set before time even began."

****

As the sun dipped lower, bathing the Mount of Olives in golden light, Grandpa Joe stood and looked at the children. "Children, remember this: God's promises never fail. Every prophecy about Jesus came true, and every promise He has made to us will come true as well. You can trust Him with your life, with your future, and with your eternity."

Hannah smiled, her heart full of peace. "It's amazing to think that God planned all of this because He loves us."

Grandpa Joe placed a hand on her shoulder, his voice gentle. "That's right, Hannah. The Bible says, *'For God so loved the world that He gave His one and only Son, that whoever believes in Him shall not perish but have eternal life.'* Jesus is God's greatest promise fulfilled, and through Him, we have hope that will never fade."

****

As they walked slowly down the Mount of Olives, the evening breeze wrapped around them like a quiet assurance. Danny looked up at Grandpa, his voice filled with quiet resolve. "I believe it, Grandpa. I believe that Jesus is who He said He is."

Grandpa Joe smiled, his eyes glistening. "That's the most important thing you'll ever believe, Danny-boy. Hold onto that truth, because it's a truth that changes everything."

Hannah looked back at the Mount of Olives, her voice soft. "God's plan really is perfect, isn't it?"

"Yes, Hannah," Grandpa Joe replied. "Perfect in every way. And the best part is, the story isn't over. One day, Jesus will return, just as He promised. And when He does, we will see the fulfillment of every promise—forever."

As they continued down the path, the golden light of evening seemed to whisper across the hills:

"God's promises are true. Jesus has come. And He is coming again."

CHAPTER 38: DANNY'S QUESTIONS ANSWERED

The sun was setting over the rolling hills of Jerusalem, painting the sky with shades of orange, pink, and gold. Danny, Hannah, and Grandpa Joe sat on a small stone ledge, overlooking the city. The golden dome of the Temple Mount gleamed in the distance, and the soft hum of the city below seemed to quiet as the evening settled in.

Grandpa Joe rested his hands on his walking stick, his gaze fixed on the horizon. The moment felt still, as if time itself had paused to listen. Danny, who had been quiet for most of the day, finally broke the silence.

"Grandpa," he began, his voice low and hesitant, "I've been thinking about everything we've seen—Bethlehem, Galilee, the cross, the empty tomb—and I... I think I believe it."

Grandpa Joe turned to look at him, his face glowing with warmth. "That's wonderful, Danny-boy. Tell me what you mean."

Danny looked down at the stone beneath his feet, gathering his thoughts. "At first, I thought Jesus was just... a good teacher, someone who did a lot of nice things for people. But after hearing all the stories, seeing the places He walked, and learning what He did on the cross... it's different now. It's real. I think Jesus really is who He said He is."

****

Grandpa Joe's eyes shone, and his voice softened with reverence. "Danny, you've come to the most important decision anyone can ever make. Believing in Jesus isn't just about knowing the stories—it's about trusting that what He did on the cross was for *you*. It's personal."

Danny glanced up. "That's the part I don't really get, Grandpa. I know Jesus died to save us, but why did He have to die? Couldn't God just... forgive us?"

Grandpa Joe leaned forward, his voice gentle but full of conviction. "That's a question many people ask, Danny, and it's one of the most important questions there is. You see, God is holy and perfect. He created us to know Him, to love Him, and to live in relationship with Him. But when sin entered the world, it created a barrier between us and God—a barrier we could never break on our own."

Hannah, who had been listening quietly, whispered, "Sin is what separates us from God, isn't it?"

"Yes, Hannah," Grandpa Joe said, nodding. "Sin isn't just the bad things we do—it's a condition of the heart. It's when we choose to live our way instead of God's way. And because God is holy, sin has to be dealt with. The Bible says, *'For the wages of sin is death, but the gift of God is eternal life in Christ Jesus our Lord.'*"

****

Danny frowned, his voice uncertain. "So... someone had to pay for it?"

Grandpa Joe nodded solemnly. "That's right, Danny. God is both just and merciful. His justice demands that sin be punished, but His love for us is so great that He provided the way to save us. That's why Jesus came. Jesus lived a perfect, sinless life, and on the cross, He took our place. He paid the penalty for our sins so we could be forgiven."

Danny looked up, his eyes searching Grandpa's face. "But why would He do that, Grandpa? Why would He die for me?"

Grandpa Joe's voice trembled slightly with emotion as he answered. "Because He loves you, Danny. More than you can ever imagine. The Bible says, *'For God so loved the world that He gave His one and only Son, that whoever believes in Him shall not perish but have eternal life.'* Jesus didn't go to the cross because He had to—He went because He wanted to. He chose the nails. He chose the pain. He chose the cross... for you."

****

The words hung in the air like a holy hush. Danny blinked hard, his voice barely above a whisper. "He really did that for me?"

"Yes, Danny-boy," Grandpa Joe said, his voice strong but tender. "When Jesus cried out, 'It is finished,' on the cross, He wasn't just talking about His suffering—He was talking about your debt. He paid it in full so you could be forgiven, so you could know God, and so you could have eternal life."

Danny sat silently for a moment, staring at the setting sun as if seeing it for the first time. "So... I don't have to earn God's love? I don't have to be perfect to be saved?"

Grandpa Joe smiled, his eyes glistening. "No, Danny. You don't have to earn it. Salvation is a gift. The Bible says, *'It is by grace you have been saved, through faith—and this is not from yourselves, it is the gift of God—not by works, so that no one can boast.'* All you have to do is believe, trust in Jesus, and accept what He's done for you."

****

Danny let out a long breath, as though a weight had been lifted from his shoulders. "I believe, Grandpa. I really do."

Grandpa Joe beamed, his face full of joy. "That's the greatest decision you'll ever make, Danny. Jesus said, *'Whoever hears My word and believes Him who sent Me has eternal life and will not be judged but has crossed over from death to life.'* That's what's happened to you, Danny-boy. You've crossed over into life—

eternal life with Jesus."

****

Hannah smiled at her brother, her voice soft but confident. "I believe, too, Grandpa. I've always known God loves us, but now it feels... deeper. Like He's with us every moment."

Grandpa Joe nodded, his voice steady. "That's because He is, Hannah. Jesus promised, *'I am with you always, to the very end of the age.'* No matter where you go or what you face, He will never leave you. He walks beside you every step of the way."

****

The three of them sat quietly, the peace of the moment settling deep into their hearts. Finally, Danny spoke, his voice full of resolve. "I want to live for Him, Grandpa. I want to tell other people what He did for us."

Grandpa Joe smiled, his voice filled with gratitude and hope. "That's what we're called to do, Danny. Jesus didn't save us so we could keep it to ourselves—He saved us so we could share His love with the world. The Great Commission we talked about is for *you*, too. Go and tell others about Jesus. Share the good news of His love, His forgiveness, and His victory over sin and death."

****

As the sun finally disappeared below the horizon, Danny looked up, his heart full and his mind at peace. "So Jesus really is alive. And He's with us."

"Yes, Danny," Grandpa Joe said, his voice firm and joyful. "He's alive, and because He lives, we have hope that never fades. Hold onto that truth, and let it guide you through every moment of your life."

****

The evening breeze wrapped gently around them as they stood to leave, the city of Jerusalem glowing softly in the distance. Danny took Grandpa Joe's hand, his voice strong and clear. "Thank you, Grandpa, for helping me understand."

Grandpa Joe squeezed his hand, his eyes shining. "Thank Jesus, Danny-boy. He's the One who did it all."

As they walked back down the path, the stars began to appear one by one in the night sky, like tiny reminders of God's perfect plan. And in that moment, Danny knew his life would never be the same—because he believed.

CHAPTER 39: HANNAH'S REFLECTION

The evening air was cool and peaceful as Hannah, Danny, and Grandpa Joe sat on a low stone wall overlooking the quiet city of Jerusalem. The stars began to emerge one by one, dotting the darkening sky like countless promises whispered by God. The day had been full, but now everything was still—a perfect moment for reflection.

Hannah hugged her knees to her chest, her face thoughtful as she gazed at the city. Grandpa Joe watched her, leaning on his walking stick, his warm smile encouraging her to speak.

"What's on your mind, sweetheart?" Grandpa asked softly.

Hannah didn't answer right away. She let the silence linger for a moment as she looked out across the Holy City. Finally, she spoke, her voice quiet but sure. "I've been thinking about everything we've seen, Grandpa. All the places we've been, all the stories you've told us. It's like… it's like I can see God's love everywhere now."

****

Danny turned to look at his sister, curious. "What do you mean, Hannah?"

Hannah glanced at him, her eyes shining. "Well, before this trip, I knew about Jesus—I knew He loved us because He died on the cross. But now it feels so much bigger than that. I see God's love in everything. From the manger in Bethlehem to the Sea of Galilee, from the Mount of Beatitudes to the cross… every single part of Jesus' life shows how much God loves us."

Grandpa Joe nodded, his face glowing with pride. "You're beginning to understand something very important, Hannah. God's love isn't just a feeling—it's an action. The Bible says, *'God demonstrates His own love for us in this: While we were still sinners, Christ died for us.'* Everything Jesus did—every word He spoke, every miracle He performed, and every step He took toward the cross—was because of God's love."

****

Hannah smiled faintly, still looking out at the city. "I think I really felt it in the Garden of Gethsemane, when you told us how Jesus prayed, 'Not my will, but Yours.' I couldn't stop thinking about how hard that must have been for Him. He could have said no, but He chose to go through it all—for us."

Grandpa Joe's voice was soft but filled with reverence. "Yes, Hannah. In that garden, Jesus made the greatest decision in history. He surrendered to the will of His Father because He loves us. He chose the cross to save us from sin and bring us back to God. That's the kind of love the world had never seen before, and it's the kind of love that changes everything."

****

Hannah continued, her voice growing stronger. "And when we visited the Mount of Beatitudes, I realized something else. Jesus taught us what God's Kingdom really looks like. It's not about power or riches—it's about love, kindness, and humility. He cared for the poor, the outcasts, the sick, and the hurting. He cared about *everyone*. And that makes me want to be more like Him."

Danny nodded slowly. "Yeah. Grandpa said that's what being a disciple is—following Jesus and living like Him."

Grandpa Joe smiled, his eyes shining with joy. "That's exactly right, Danny. You see, Hannah, what you're describing is the heart of the gospel. God's love isn't just something we receive—it's something we share. Jesus told us, *'A new command I give you: Love one another. As I have loved you, so you must love one another.'* When we understand the depth of God's love for us, it changes the way we see the world, and it changes the way we treat others."

****

Hannah looked up, her face glowing with a quiet confidence. "That's what I want to do, Grandpa. I want to love people the way Jesus does. I want to help others see how much He cares about them."

Grandpa Joe beamed, his voice gentle but full of conviction. "That's the most important thing you can do, Hannah. Jesus' love is the light that shines in the darkness. And you can carry that light wherever you go—at home, at school, wherever God places you. The Bible says, *'Let your light shine before others, that they may see your good deeds and glorify your Father in heaven.'*"

****

Danny looked at his sister, grinning slightly. "So you're saying this trip changed you?"

Hannah nodded, her voice steady. "It did. Before, I thought God's love was just something we talked about at church. But now I see it everywhere—in the Bible, in Jesus' life, and even in the people we've met here. God's love is real, and it's for everyone."

She paused, looking back at Grandpa Joe. "I think the biggest thing I've learned is that God never stops loving us. Even when we mess up, even when we doubt, He's still there. Jesus didn't just die for people back then—He died for us, for me, for everyone. And because He rose again, we can have hope no matter what."

****

Grandpa Joe's eyes glistened as he listened. "Hannah, you're right. The love of God never fails. It's the kind of love that sent Jesus to the cross, and it's the kind of love that brings us back to Him. It's a love that forgives, redeems, and restores. And when we accept that love, we can't help but share it with others."

Hannah smiled, her heart full. "I want to share it, Grandpa. I want people to see Jesus through the way I live."

Grandpa Joe placed a gentle hand on her shoulder, his voice full of warmth. "That's the call of every believer, Hannah. Jesus told us to *'go and make disciples of all nations.'* And sometimes that starts with the people right around us—our family, our friends, even strangers who need a little kindness."

****

The three of them sat in quiet reflection as the stars above them multiplied, shining brightly against the deepening night sky. Danny spoke softly, his voice thoughtful. "So, God's love isn't just something we keep for ourselves?"

"No, Danny," Grandpa Joe replied. "God's love is meant to be shared. It's the greatest gift we could ever receive, and the greatest gift we can ever give. You see, children, the world is full of people searching for hope, peace, and meaning. But only Jesus can satisfy the longing of their hearts. And when we live as His disciples, we get to point people to Him."

****

Hannah smiled, looking out over Jerusalem. "It feels like this trip was just the beginning, Grandpa."

Grandpa Joe grinned, his face lit with joy. "It is, Hannah. The journey of faith never ends. Each day is an opportunity to grow closer to God, to experience His love, and to share it with the world. And as long as you keep your eyes on Jesus, He will guide you every step of the way."

****

As they stood to leave, Grandpa Joe looked at his grandchildren with pride and gratitude. "Children, remember this: God's love is the greatest story ever told. Jesus' life, death, and resurrection show us just how much He cares for us. And when you know that truth, when it settles deep in your heart, it changes everything."

Hannah took Grandpa's hand and smiled up at him. "I think it already has, Grandpa."

As they walked back down the path, the stars above seemed brighter than ever, like tiny beacons of God's love scattered across the heavens. And in her heart, Hannah knew that she would never see the world the same way again—because now, she could see God's love everywhere.

CHAPTER 40: HOME AGAIN, FOREVER CHANGED

The early morning sun streamed through the kitchen window as the smell of freshly baked quiche and freshly brewed coffee filled the house. Laughter echoed down the hallway as Danny and Hannah helped set the table, their steps light and faces glowing. It was Easter Sunday—back home in their familiar surroundings—but something was different. The house felt the same, yet their hearts had been forever changed.

Grandpa Joe sat in his favorite chair by the window, his Bible resting on his lap as he quietly reflected. Outside, the trees had begun to bloom, as if creation itself was celebrating the day. He looked up and smiled as Danny came in, carrying a stack of plates.

"Morning, Danny-boy," Grandpa said warmly.

Danny grinned. "Good morning, Grandpa! Mom's making sure everything is perfect for Easter lunch."

Grandpa chuckled. "That's what Easter's about, Danny—not perfection on our table, but the perfect victory Jesus won for us."

****

Hannah appeared next, carrying silverware and a bright vase of spring flowers. "Everything looks so alive this morning," she said, glancing outside. "It's like the whole world knows it's Easter."

Grandpa Joe's smile deepened as he leaned forward, his voice rich with warmth. "That's because Easter *is* a celebration of life, Hannah. Jesus conquered sin and death when He rose from the grave. That's not just good news—it's the best news the world has ever heard."

****

As the table came together, the family gathered around— Danny, Hannah, their parents, and Grandpa Joe. The prayer before the meal carried a weight and a gratitude that was new to them all. Grandpa Joe bowed his head, his voice steady and reverent.

"Heavenly Father, we come before You today, humbled and grateful for the gift of Easter. Thank You for sending Your Son, Jesus Christ, to die for our sins and to rise again, giving us the hope of eternal life. Lord, You are faithful to Your promises, and Your love never fails. Help us to live for You, to share Your light with others, and to remember the victory of this day. In Jesus' name, amen."

"Amen," everyone echoed, their voices unified in gratitude.

****

As they began eating, the conversation turned to their trip. Danny, who had been quiet until now, spoke up. "You know, I didn't really understand Easter before. I thought it was just about going to church and having a nice dinner." He looked over at Grandpa. "But now I know it's so much more. Jesus really did all of this... for us."

Grandpa Joe nodded, his eyes shining. "That's right, Danny-boy. Easter isn't just a story—it's the truth that changes everything. The empty tomb means that death is not the end. It means hope, life, and victory for all who believe."

****

Hannah set down her fork, her voice soft but clear. "I used to think God's love was just something we talked about in church, but now I see it everywhere. Jesus' life, His death, and His resurrection—they're proof that God's love never fails."

Their mother smiled at Hannah, her voice full of warmth. "It's amazing how one journey can change your perspective."

Grandpa Joe's face beamed with joy as he looked at his family. "That's because this journey wasn't just about seeing places—it was about seeing Jesus. God gave us the greatest gift when He sent His Son to save us, and when we truly understand that, it changes everything. It changes how we see the world, how we see each other, and how we live."

****

Danny leaned back in his chair, his expression thoughtful. "Grandpa, you always said that faith isn't just knowing the stories—it's about believing them. I think I finally get it now. Jesus really is alive, and that changes everything."

Grandpa Joe's voice grew soft, his words rich with meaning. "Yes, Danny. That's the heart of the gospel. Jesus is alive, and because He lives, we have hope that will never fade. The Bible says, *'Because I live, you also will live.'* That's His promise to us. Death has no hold on those who believe in Him."

****

The room grew quiet for a moment, the truth of Grandpa's words settling deep into their hearts. Finally, their father spoke, his voice firm but gentle. "It's easy to forget what really matters in the middle of life's busyness. But today, I'm reminded that Easter isn't just one day on the calendar. It's the foundation of our faith."

Hannah smiled, glancing over at Danny. "It's like Grandpa said—when we understand what Jesus did, we can't keep it to ourselves. We have to share it with others."

Grandpa Joe beamed, his heart full. "That's right, Hannah. Jesus told us to *'go and make disciples of all nations.'* The good news of Easter is too important to keep quiet. It's a message of hope for the whole world."

****

As the meal wrapped up, they moved into the living room, where the sunlight poured through the windows. Grandpa Joe sat back in his chair, his Bible still open on his lap, as Danny and Hannah sat cross-legged on the rug.

"Children," Grandpa said, his voice steady and full of joy, "the resurrection of Jesus is the promise of eternal life. But it's also a promise for today. Jesus is with us—right now. He walks with us through every joy, every trial, and every moment in between. And because He lives, we can face tomorrow with confidence and peace."

Danny nodded, his voice full of resolve. "I believe it, Grandpa. Jesus is alive, and He's with us."

Hannah smiled softly. "Me too. And I want to live my life in a way that shows others how much He loves them."

Grandpa Joe's face lit up, his eyes glistening. "That's all He asks of us, children—to believe in Him, to trust Him, and to share His love with the world. When we do that, we are living out the victory of Easter every day."

****

The room filled with a peaceful stillness as the family sat together, grateful for the journey that had changed them. Outside, the sun dipped lower on the horizon, casting its golden light across the earth.

As Danny looked out the window, he whispered to himself, "He is risen."

Hannah smiled, hearing him, and softly echoed the words: "He is risen, indeed."

Grandpa Joe nodded, his voice quiet but strong. "And because He lives, we can live, too—forever changed."

****

The family gathered for one final prayer, their hearts full of gratitude and joy. As Grandpa Joe prayed, his words seemed to carry the truth of the journey:

"Lord, thank You for this day, for Your sacrifice, and for the victory of the resurrection. Thank You for changing our hearts and showing us what it means to walk with You. Help us to live with bold faith, to share Your love, and to never forget the hope we have in Jesus. In His name we pray. Amen."

"Amen," the family echoed together, their voices steady and full of peace.

****

As the evening settled and the stars appeared in the sky, Danny and Hannah knew that this Easter would stay with them forever. They had walked where Jesus walked, heard His story, and come to know His love in a deeper way. And now, as they returned to the rhythms of home, they carried with them a faith that would guide them for the rest of their lives.

For Jesus was alive—**and because He lives, everything is forever changed.**

www.ingramcontent.com/pod-product-compliance
Lightning Source LLC
Chambersburg PA
CBHW070748180626
46818CB00007B/3039